'*Riambel* bravel\
Mauritius . . . d
with indignation and in the gaps in what is not said.'

J. M. G. LE CLÉZIO,
winner of the Nobel Prize for Literature

'Priya Hein's novel is spellbinding. *Riambel* is beautiful. It is terse and yet lyrical. It is tough, and yet bursting with life. Set in the reality of a young girl, while also in her imaginary world, the novel has its own aura and even its own momentum, the writer's own imagination carrying the reader forward. With this her first novel, Priya Hein contributes to unifying an emerging, bubbling new Mauritian literature. *Riambel* is a feat that transports us into the inner being of a teenager, awakening us to what the world was from the time of slavery, what it still is today, and even to what it might have been, thus what it might be.'

LINDSEY COLLEN,
author of *The Rape of Sita*

'With *Riambel*, Priya Hein has given us a book that should be essential reading for all those who care about our history, in particular the devastating legacy of slavery; but what is extraordinary is that she tells this harrowing story in the most beautiful prose, luminous and musical, drawing in the reader before hitting them hard with the reality of her young narrator's life, and the humiliations and pain she endures because of this very legacy. Today more than ever, this story needs to be told; Priya Hein does so movingly and powerfully.'

ANANDA DEVI,
author of *Eve Out of Her Ruins*

'I was astounded by the blistering prose and originality in Priya Hein's stunning debut *Riambel* . . . Against the backdrop of uncomfortable and, at times, disturbing fragments depicting abuse, rape and exploitation, I loved the way the richness of the local Mauritians' culture is depicted: through culinary recipes, oral history, poetry and songs woven beautifully into the narrative. It's a slim novel but one that punches deeply and screams aloud. It invites us to oppose the injustice of the longstanding structures of class, hostility and white capitalism.'

NATALIYA DELEVA,
author of *Arrival*

'A stunning book which cradles the anger of generational slavery experienced by Mauritians. These topics are usually swept under the carpet in Mauritian households as it is a history that brings much shame, however the recipes within this book provide a literary pause within the pain to remember the warmth of familiar comforting recipes which any child of Mauritius would relate to, irrespective of how their lineage is defined. Gato Pima, Kat Kat and Kari Krevet provide warmth and the memory of a mother's love within the tragedy of institutionalised racism . . . thank you Priya for sharing our history with the world.'

SHELINA PERMALLOO,
Food Writer and TV Chef

'In the span of a mere 160 pages, this extraordinary debut packs rare insight into the trauma and deference seeded by the long reign of capitalism and the white man's whims.'

VARTIKA RASTOGI,
*The Cardiff Review*

'Modern and edgy . . . rich in smells, sounds and feelings.'
*Süddeutsche Zeitung*

THE
INDIGO
PRESS

# RIAMBEL

# RIAMBEL

PRIYA HEIN

THE
INDIGO
PRESS

THE INDIGO PRESS
50 Albemarle Street
London W1S 4BD
www.theindigopress.com

The Indigo Press Publishing Limited Reg. No. 10995574
Registered Office: Wellesley House, Duke of Wellington Avenue
Royal Arsenal, London SE18 6SS

First published in Great Britain in 2023 by The Indigo Press

A CIP catalogue record for this book is available from the British Library

This is a work of fiction. Names, characters, places and incidents are
products of the author's imagination or are used fictionally and are
not to be construed as real. Any resemblance to actual events, locales,
organisations or persons, living or dead, is entirely coincidental.

ISBN: 978-1-911648-49-9
eBook ISBN: 978-1-911648-50-5

The unedited and unpublished text of this book won the Prix Jean Fanchette
2021 from the Municipality of Beau Bassin-Rose Hill (Mauritius).

Cover design © Luke Bird
Art direction by House of Thought
Front cover painting by Mila Gupta
Author photo © Florence Guillemain
Typeset by Tetragon, London
Printed and bound in Great Britain by TJ Books Limited, Padstow

*For Stefan, Ananya and Kian.*
*Thank you for taking me home.*

# AUTHOR'S NOTE

I have lived abroad for over thirty years as an immigrant. Quite often, I have been asked by the local majority to conform. But what does this word mean? The English word 'conform' means to comply with rules or standards – to be similar in form or type – to behave according to socially acceptable conventions. In French, *se conformer* means to obey and behave in accordance with pre-existing social and ideological conventions, to fit the mould.

But my question is: who imposes these rules?

I had been living and working in Germany for about two decades when George Floyd was murdered in May 2020. This brutal incident was the catalyst for Black Lives Matter protests all around the world. When I dared to speak about the racist incidents I had experienced as an immigrant (offensive comments, microaggressions, exclusion, condescension) to people I had regular interactions with, I was not taken seriously. I was told that what I had experienced was not racism, that I was being 'oversensitive' and that as an immigrant I had to accept this sort of behaviour. There was a clear lack of empathy, especially when they tried to silence and intimidate me. As a member of an ethnic minority, I was not allowed to 'complain' but was told that I should be 'grateful' and should *conform*.

So I decided to let my pen and my heart speak for themselves. I sat down during a long weekend in June 2020 and wrote the first draft of *Riambel* in a practice that was intended to be non-conformist.

Among one of the many possible origins of the word 'sugar' is the Sanskrit word 'śarkarā' meaning 'gravel' or 'grit'. This is perhaps a more appropriate term, for this is the sensation that sugar left on the palate of those forced to cultivate it. Indeed, it is generally agreed that of all cash crops, sugar has caused the most suffering upon those peoples engaged in its production and there is no better illustration of this than the Mauritian experience. Few people in Mauritius, however, recognise the traumatic side of the history of 'sugar' or are conscious of the dislocation that sugar has caused to the millions of people all over the world who were forced to cultivate it. Sugar made the fortunes of some; but it also caused untold misery to many more. Yet we continue to accept representations of the history of sugar as a heroic venture that brought prosperity to the island as a whole. There is another side to the sugar 'story' that has not been narrated.

VIJAYA TEELOCK, *Bitter Sugar*

*Certes mes pas aveugles reconnaîtraient*
*Les sables de Riambel*
*Mes pieds apprivoiseraient la terre brûlée*
*Et la mer Indienne saurait laver*
*La poussière d'Europe*
*Dans un unique sacrement d'aurore.*

Surely my blind steps would recognise
The sands of Riambel
My feet would tame the burned earth
And the Indian sea could wash away
The dust of Europe
In its own rite of dawn.

JEAN FANCHETTE, from 'Constat'
(translated by Jeffrey Zuckerman)

*I'm the great-granddaughter of plantation rape. There's a tinge to my slightly-light-ebony-blackness. I'm the daughter of Creole slaves and something far more sinister. Descendant of domestic servants and white masters who abused their workers. I have white male ancestry in me. Involuntarily. The whiteness I carry was not a choice. The greedy sugar barons took what they wanted – women and girls over whom they had extraordinary power – and then failed to claim their children. How can they deny their morbid past when we – the bastard children of colonialism – are here to remind them of their legacy? We carry the truth. As clear as daylight. The blue sky above is not a lie. We're the living proof of a dark history that cannot be whitewashed.*

*Look at me and tell me that history hasn't tainted me.*

# I

I've nurtured a special relationship with our Indian Ocean. Cradled to sleep by its motion. Wrapped in its vast blanket of blue. I am its creature. Its fluidity defines me. The sea pulses through my veins. Throbbing. Keeping me alive. Keeping me sane.

My skin is impregnated with its salty smell. Tiny grains of sand are permanently trapped beneath my toenails. I tried to remove them, but then I gave up. What's the point? Anyway, I like the idea that I'm carrying a little bit of the sea with me wherever I go.

I've known the ocean all my life. Mama says I was practically born here on this beach. The sea is in me. I feel its deep currents running in my veins. Pulsing and throbbing. Constantly. At night I hear the waves murmuring, and rocking me to sleep the way a mother and a father ought to have. And when I finally drift off to sleep its lulling wakes me up – unless the neighbours are having one of their parties.

It's in this fishing village buried in the most southern part of the island that I was born and where I have spent all fifteen years of my life. My village is called Riambel: Ri-am-bel.

Ri
Am
Bel

It has a sing-song feel to it – something that implies summer and laughter. I once asked Mama if the name of our village comes from the words *rire en belle*. To laugh wholeheartedly. Without restraint.

*Rire?* Laugh? What would I know? There's nothing to laugh about in this life – is there? Now stop all that nonsense talk and help me with the chores before you go to school. I'll be late for work. I can't afford to lose my job. Who's going to feed you?

So that was the end of that conversation.

## 2

We live in a *cité*, or *kan kreol* (which is how they like to refer to our shanty town). It's also known as Africa Town – a slum where the poor and the undesirables are dumped together in hastily constructed barracks. Like tins of sardines placed next to each other in a higgledy-piggledy way. Whatever's found in the trash somehow ends up in our *cité*, which is nothing but the waste of Riambel discarded in a heap that slowly rots away. A trash-strewn ghetto where everything is starving and fighting to survive – even the dogs.

*It's the smell that you remember the most. The odour of hundreds of men and women living on top of each other in the barracks behind the estates. Huddled together like animals in the dark with nothing but the fermenting smell of the latrine to keep you company. A hole in the ground. There are no words to describe the odour. You once had a look inside with a torch and saw thousands of fat white maggots wriggling about on heaps of shit and urine. There were other things thriving in there. Perhaps snakes. It was hard to tell in the dark. You had nightmares of falling into that hole of kaka. You sometimes close your eyes and see those white maggots burning in hell.*

# 3

From the outside, our *ti lakaz* isn't so different from all the others. There's a small fence with a rusty gate. As soon as you lift the latch, you stumble into our living room, which serves as a TV-cum-dining room, kitchen and guest room. In the corner, there's a table consisting of a concrete slab attached to the wall. Next to it is a sink with a single tap sticking out of a rusty pipe, which is always dripping. There's also a gas cooker with two hot rings.

Mama sewed together some mismatched bits of flowery cotton – now stiff with grease – to make a curtain to hide the blue gas bottle. Next to the *bobonn gaz*, our few groceries are stored in sturdy jute bags that factory workers from the estates used to carry sugar in. Mama likes to store them in those thick bags which are harder for cockroaches and the likes to penetrate, but they still manage. The nasty little pests force their way through and encroach, no matter what. Like those horrid leeches around the yard that we can never get rid of.

Since we don't own a fridge, the jute bags are sort of our cooler. Grand-père borrowed one or two from the sugar factory before they had to shut it down. On top of the sink, there's a wooden shelf with hooks where Mama hangs her few blackened pots and pans. It's not much of a kitchen, but that never stopped Marie from whipping up a mean curry!

*Tifi-la ena bon lame kwi.* The girl's got magic hands in the kitchen, Grand-mère would say, not without a sparkle in her eyes.

Mama's room leads to the outside toilet and bathroom, which is nothing more than a tiny cubicle made of coarsely plastered bricks and a creaky wooden door. On one side there is a hole in the floor, and on the other are a metal tap and a steel bucket. Once the bucket is filled, we use a small jug – *lamok* – to pour cold water over our bodies and hair as we squat on a small plastic stool made for a child. If we want to wash with hot water we first have to heat it in a big pot in the kitchen before carrying the pan outside. The whole procedure is cumbersome, especially as we don't exactly like to linger in there.

I prefer to bathe in the sea and let the ocean wash away the daily grime of the *cité*. It feels good to float in the lagoon. To let go and enjoy the sensation of being carried away by the waves and feel free, if only for a few minutes.

If I need to use the toilet at night, I have to cross Mama's room to go into the backyard or wait until the morning (especially if she has an uncle visiting). Once, one of the nicer uncles brought us a bottle of Fanta, a rare treat. Unable to resist, I added some salt to it. I watched it sizzle before gulping the whole bottle in one go. That night, I desperately had to pee. So I peed into the empty bottle with hot fury and threw out the warm orangey liquid first thing in the morning, so that I wouldn't get caught.

# 4

I always find it strange how there's only one road that divides us from them. Us. Them. *Zot. Nou. Gran Dimounn. Ti Dimounn.* Big people. Small people. On one side of the winding coastal road there are the *kanpman* and the estates of the *blan* that reek of old money, alongside the properties of the nouveau riche which face the ocean. Old summer retreats with their former slave quarters turned guest houses. But you only have to cross the road and you'll get to see the real Mauritius. Merely a few metres away. The side they won't show you on the postcards and the glossy brochures that are used as bait to lure excited tourists to our paradise island, to unleash bundles of euro notes from their chunky wallets – not that we ever get to see any of it.

For as long as I can remember, Mama's been working as a maid in one of those houses across the road. Serving the same white family as her parents. The De Grandbourg family – white Franco-Mauritians who like to boast of an ancestry that goes all the way back to a château in Brittany. De Grandbourg. Ha! Even their name denotes big. Grand.

My favourite teacher says that the Mauritian *blan* probably descend from peasants, mere blacksmiths and lowly sailors. Franco-Mauritians like to tell little white lies about their seemingly blue blood, having made their fortune from the slave trade. To wash their bloody hands. But will they ever be able to clean their tarnished souls?

Grand-mère used to say that dark deeds always come to light.

# 5

There are some small differences that set our *ti lakaz* apart from the others in the *cité*. Mama occasionally brings little trinkets home from work. Nothing that would raise suspicion. She would never steal and risk losing her job. No. Just small things that no one will miss. A sliver of lavender soap from a chunky bar of Savon de Marseille that she surreptitiously slips into her bra when no one's looking. The odd can of corned beef, or a handful of Prince Lu biscuits wrapped in old newspaper sheets that mysteriously find their way into the depths of her pocket.

They also give Mama things they no longer have any use for: some colouring crayons for my crude sketches. Scraps of paper for my scribblings, a rag of words. Torn copies of *Paris Match* with outdated pictures of European princesses waving at an adoring crowd, which I devour. A teddy bear with a missing eye. And things that are still serviceable in our household: a slightly stained tablecloth. Old cotton sheets frayed along the edges. A dainty teapot that has lost its handle. A wooden cupboard without a door. A colourful dress that has shrunk in the wash. These little 'gifts' make our *ti lakaz* by far the nicest.

# 6

Mama doesn't like it when I walk barefoot outside the house. When I was about eight years old I used to love playing with the earth – digging and stabbing the mud with a bamboo stick – and climbing trees. One day, I clambered onto the branches of the zanbalak tree, trying to reach the roof of our barracks. But just before reaching the top of the tree, I felt something dangling from the back of my short cotton dress. I absent-mindedly brushed it away, but it started to crawl on my skin. Thinking that the ribbons of my dress had come undone, I tried to reach the back in order to tie them. Instead I felt something warm and slippery in my hands. As I pulled I felt a slight pressure on my lower back – something moist sliding out from between my buttocks.

Marie looked at my hands and started screaming at the top of her lungs. I was holding a long, slippery pink worm that was still alive. Terrified, I tried to let go of it by throwing it away, but it still hung from my itchy bum, wriggling against my thighs. Mama ran out to see what was happening. Taking one look at me with my legs spread wide apart, she quickly turned me around and lifted my dress. I was wailing and shaking as she pulled the dangly worm out of my arse. It was almost one metre long.

I still have nightmares of long pinkish creatures coming out of my intestines to wrap themselves around my neck. Like angry pink hands. Sausage fingers. Strangling me. Closing my windpipe until my throat judders. Tightening like a choke collar, silencing me. Suffocating me. Choking me to death.

*Help, Mama! I can't breathe.*

# KAT-KAT MANIOK
## (CASSAVA STEW)

So you want to how to make a dish like the ones the former slaves would eat? My Grand-mère used to make the best *kat-kat maniok* on the entire island – back in the slaves' barracks, her coarse hands raw and wrinkled from years of laborious work.

Once you've pulled your cassava plants from the earth, choose two to three decent-sized roots and wash all the dirt off. Peel and cut into chunks, before putting the pieces in a big pan of water to cook over the fire. Add some sea salt and leave to simmer until the cassavas are tender. Make sure they are thoroughly cooked, otherwise you'll upset your stomach. Remove from the fire. Drain and leave to cool. Meanwhile, fry some chopped onions and crushed garlic paste in a little bit of oil. Add the cassava pieces to the pan with chunks of fresh tuna or marlin and fry gently for a few minutes. Throw in some fresh curry leaves and stir. Pour some coconut milk into the pan and let it simmer until creamy and the cassava pieces start to melt into a thick sauce. Sprinkle with salt and crushed black pepper and a bunch of thyme. Add in a handful of wild red peppercorns that grow abundantly in the forests near Le Morne Brabant mountain where the runaway slaves – *esklav maron* – used to hide from their masters. Serve on its own as a stew or with bread.

# 7

Grand-mère used to sing us lullabies passed down from her mother. Her voice was as soft as the murmur of the waves. When she sang her skin would gently ripple like wind over water.

*Mo pase larivier Taniers*
*Mo zwenn enn vie gran mama*
*Mo dir li ki li fer la*
*Li dir mwa li lapes kabo*
*Wai wai, me zanfan*
*Fo travay pou gagn son pin*
*Wai wai, me zanfan*
*Fo travay pou gagn son pin*

I pass by Taniers river
I meet an old grandmother
I ask her what she's doing there
She tells me she's fishing
Alas, alas, my children
We must work to earn our crust
Alas, alas, my children
We must work to earn our crust

# 8

Mama worked all hours of the day and sometimes also at night, when they had one of their famous soirées where high society, the white Franco-Mauritians, gathered.

Marie and I were often left alone, so we wandered along the beach. To watch the fishermen or to play with the other *cité* kids. We would swim in the sea every day, and if we didn't we were like fish out of water.

Look at you two! As if your hair isn't dry and frizzy enough as it is. All that salty water and sea breeze will only make it worse. Your hair's like dry coconut strings.

Marie and I couldn't care less about the state of our nestlike hair that would break combs if we tried taming it.

Not even bad weather could stop us from submerging ourselves in the lagoon and letting ourselves be carried away by the sea. Unless the man we used to call Père or Per gave us a good beating with his belt. We patiently waited a few days before letting the waves wash away the pain of our freshly torn skin before running into the ocean again with new scars. We would rush into the lagoon with our arms outstretched – about to hug the water. Like a reunion with a long-lost friend.

Last we heard, Per was on the island of Rodrigues fishing for octopus. He had managed to escape there on a boat before he got arrested for some crime that Mama doesn't like to talk about. He'll be sent to jail if he comes back, so he's better off there hiding among the fisherfolk somewhere near Port Mathurin.

Good riddance, says Mama whenever she talks about him, with a look of disgust on her face. Now I don't have to hand over all my earnings to that *vilin soular bonarien*. Good-for-nothing.

I never again want to see him swagger into our room reeking of cheap rum and tobacco while undoing his belt.

# 9

Since Marie left us I have no one to bathe in the sea with. The days feel longer without her. After school I like to sit on the shore, reading and staring at the ocean. I watch how the sea breeze makes ripples in the ocean. It doesn't make big waves, but just a gentle stir on the surface of the water. Like a candle being blown. Quiet but still noticeable.

Sometimes when I look out at the ocean, I want to swim as far towards the horizon as I can manage.

*Even at night you're not free. There are regular visits from the masters and their sons. They come in and point towards a girl or a woman. She's expected to follow Ti Patron or Gran Patron in the dark – subdued. Like a lamb. One night, a little girl of about ten is picked. Her eyes still sleepy, having been snatched from her childish dreams.*

*Hours later – at the crack of dawn – we hear her limp back into the barracks. She has no clothes on. There are fingerprint bruises on her neck. And red rings around her wrists and ankles, as if she'd been tied down. She whimpers in the darkness like a wounded animal. The practice of breaking a young horse, training it to be ridden, to make sure it knows how to be responsive to its owner. A trail of blood in the dark. A broken hymen.*

# I O

Mama says I should stop daydreaming and give her a hand with the household chores.

Madame asked me to come extra early today, so I could really do with your help. I'm talking to you, Noemi! she says pointedly, while eyeing the dirty mess in the sink.

With a sigh I open the rusty tap and let the water run over the greasy dishes.

You'd better do it quick before they turn the water off. Otherwise you'll have to wait until the evening and the *kankrela pou donn enn bal*. The cockroaches will throw a party.

As if they haven't already, I mumble.

What was that?

Nothing.

I squirt some green detergent which Mama dilutes with water and fresh lemon to make it last longer. And I start sponging off the chicken gravy from last night's dinner. A rare treat given our usual lentils with *rougay* and rice. I try not to think about those little *kankrela* feasting on the bits of carcass stuck to the dirty dishes.

Now that school's almost over you'd better stop all that gallivanting on the beach, Mama says as she opens her compact powder and dabs a sponge all over her face. The whitish powder looks like ash on her nose and cheeks.

I asked Madame if you could come and give a hand during the holidays. She said you could help in the kitchen. With the help of a tissue, Mama brushes away the excess powder and then adds some blush to her cheeks before applying lipstick. I could

34

really use the extra cash to buy a fridge, now that the abominable December heat's approaching. They'll be on sale just before Christmas. But no need to wait for the school break. You can start tomorrow.

I shrug and place the clean plates upside down on a blue plastic tray that's seen better days.

Her daughter and family are coming over from Australia for her seventieth birthday, she moans. It's going to be a big celebration. You know what they are like! There will be so much to do in that big house of theirs! She doesn't even wait for an answer. The gate creaks behind her as she practically runs down the road holding on to her *panier*.

What could I say? As if I had a choice. I pick up my bag and lock the door behind me. Sometimes I wonder why I even bother, when anyone with a hairpin could pick the flimsy lock, but then again, who would steal from us? What's there to steal from a single mother and her lanky teenage daughter? An ancient TV? Our broken furniture? Oh no. They are better off breaking into gated *pieds dans l'eau* properties after being tipped off by insiders. Once or twice, a gang tried to blackmail Mama into giving them information about the De Grandbourg family, but Mama wouldn't budge. There's something that ties her to them. She'll always remain loyal to that family – no matter what. So in the end they got the information from their security guard instead. Strange, that the ones who are supposed to be guarding their bosses' properties are the first ones to talk – as long as they get their share. You can buy just about anything around here.

## KARI KREVET
## (PRAWN CURRY)

Make sure that your prawns are fresh by checking their colour. They should look transparent and smell of the sea. Give them a quick rinse in cold water. Pull off their heads, tails and legs before removing the shells and the black veins. Once this is done, rinse the prawns again under cold water. Using a *ros kari* or a stone mortar, crush some garlic cloves together with a small finger of fresh ginger. Pour a little oil in a pan and fry the paste over a medium fire. Add one chopped onion and continue to fry until golden. Throw in your prawns and cook for a couple of minutes. Add one or two chopped tomatoes and one sliced chilli and stir. Throw in some masala and a few curry leaves. Don't make it too spicy for the whites, otherwise they'll complain about their delicate stomachs. Stir well until it thickens. Add a little sea salt, but not too much, as the prawns are already salty. Pour in a dash of water if needed. Sprinkle with fresh coriander and serve with pickled vegetables – *enn ti zasar legim* – and freshly cooked rice.

# I I

On my way to school, I carefully tread over a confetti of petals blown loose by the tropical rain. The morning air is filled with the promise of summer.

The frangipanis in the playground are beginning to blossom. Delicately. Slowly unfurling. One by one. Yearning. Gracefully stretching towards the blue sky above.

Pure and white as hope.

It's unbearably hot outside, but I don't have a long way to walk. Our village's community school is not big but I like it there. It's much nicer than some of the other nearby schools, which are nothing more than slabs of depressing grey cement that look like prisons. Ours is named after a famous poet who used to live in a little village near Riambel called Souillac. *Robert Edward Hart Secondary School* is neatly written on the wall. I like looking at it every morning before entering the courtyard with a little sense of pride, for he was someone important, and a very good poet in my humble opinion. With school, we once visited his former beach cottage made of coral, which has now been turned into a museum. From there, he wrote about the mystical ocean – of mermaids and filao trees dancing to the sweet melody of the Indian sea.

Our school sounds posh even though it isn't. It's not like the grand schools or the fancy colonial buildings that house schools, like the Couvent de Lorette that I once walked past in Curepipe. No, it's nothing like that. Most of the teachers who work here look harassed. They say that youngsters nowadays are full of *koler*. Angst. But it's actually the other way round. It's the teachers who

37

seem to be angry at us. Or just plain bored. They are idling away their days until they can finally retire and fulfil their lifelong dream of owning a tax-free Toyota – one of the perks of being a government official. As if it's our fault that they ended up being posted to this godforsaken part of the island where nothing much ever happens. But there are one or two teachers who are nice enough. The younger ones, like Misie Ravindranath, who says we should call him Misie Ravi. His namesake suits him, for he is always *ravi*.

Smiling.

*Ravi*.

Even when there's nothing to smile about. Wherever he goes, he carries with him a tattered satchel that smells of soft, warm leather. The way he holds on to it suggests that it contains things of great value, but I happen to know that he only carries a notebook that he's always scribbling into – whenever he has a spare moment – and a small stainless steel *katori* containing his lunch. Not that he eats much. He doesn't seem to have time for food. He's skinny as a stick, but there's a glow in his eyes, especially when he talks about Mauritian authors or when he tells us stories about Mama Lanatir or Père Laval. One day, he lent me a battered copy of *Les Fleurs du mal* by Charles Baudelaire, whose poems had been inspired by Mauritius.

He had asked me what I like to read and why. Anything and everything, I had said, shyly. I read because it allows me to travel and discover places I can only dream of. To open a book is like diving into an ocean glimmering with promises.

The next day, Misie Ravi awarded me an A for my short essay. My heart was close to bursting with pride.

# 12

I went to the De Grandbourgs' residence a few times, when I was smaller, while Mama worked her weekend shift. I wasn't allowed to touch anything or say anything. That was the rule. So I sat quietly under the shade of a badamier tree at the back of the *lakour*, where Mama could still keep an eye on me through the open kitchen door. Every now and then, she would leave her chores and bring me some fresh coconut water which we'd drink together from a small plastic cup. Maids are not allowed to use glassware from the household.

There is a corner in the outside kitchen where the servants store things – not far from the dog cage. That's where Mama keeps her chipped plate and a rusty spoon as well as the plastic cup that we shared. If no one was about, she would slip a strawberry jam sandwich into my little brown hand and hide a piece in her apron to give to Marie afterwards.

Eat it quickly and wipe your mouth so there are no telltale signs, she would say.

I always had the horrible sensation of being watched. Maybe because of the house's proximity to the sailors' cemetery – an eerie place of worship of all kinds.

Mama calls her boss Madame La Reine or Madame, but only when she's feeling generous. Otherwise she refers to her as the Old Bat. I don't know where she got the nickname of La Reine, but it rather suits her. Even in her fragile state, there's something majestic and stern about her. When she speaks, the whole household hangs on to her every word.

I once saw a picture of her on her wedding day. She looked just like the glamorous princesses from the old copies of *Paris Match*.

*Everyone is locked in their own darkness. A shadow begins to expand. The sound of your breathing surprises you. Other faint noises can be heard behind the pounding of your temples – echoes of muffled steps, creaking of doors half-closed, whispers. Voices and words of a bygone era grow louder and ricochet around the room, foreshadowing an impending storm before exploding.*

# 1 3

I used to sit on Grand-mère's lap when she was still alive. She'd remove her headscarf and let me play with her hair while I pretended I was combing my doll's hair. My soft doll didn't have hair, but strings of wool that would fall off in cotton-like lumps if I pulled too hard. Grand-mère's grey hair wasn't long, but it was as strong as wire.

Together we'd comb the beach at low tide, looking for *bigorno* near the rocks lined with broken shells. She'd carry me on her hips so my little feet wouldn't get cut, although she'd be walking barefoot. The sea urchins with their needle-like spikes moving about creepily didn't seem to bother Grand-mère – neither did the ugly sea cucumbers. Sometimes, she would close her eyes listening to the waves, her leathery face beaten by salt and wind.

I liked watching her mash overripe bananas, mixed with flour and a splash of milk, to make *beignets* – *gato banann* – sweet banana fritters as warm as the day.

Noemi, you eat like a bird, she'd tease me. Her toothless smile and her twinkling eyes reminded me of stars in a sky free of clouds.

After washing my hair, she would rub my head and body with coconut oil. I could feel her rough hands full of scabs and calluses from years of slaving away. Hands as coarse as grains of brown sugar before it is refined into a white powder.

When I was sad I'd cling to her and inhale her salty smell that reminded me of the sea. Like a little monkey, I'd wrap my arms and legs around her softness. After she died peacefully in her sleep there was no one for me to hold on to.

# 14

At three o'clock sharp, I walk down the coastal road just after the public beach and meet Mama in front of the gate. Without a word, she ushers me through the back door – the servants' entrance – into the kitchen. I remove my sandals and leave them next to Mama's Dodo flip-flops on the stone steps. Dirty brown feet should not soil the pristine houses of the whites.

I have to finish serving La Reine her tea before it gets cold. Madame has guests, Mama tells me. You stay here and don't touch anything until I come back. And wear this. She throws an apron at me.

With her frizzy hair tied back in a bandana, Mama looks good in her neat uniform – like Marie used to. She picks up the wooden tray full of dainty porcelain and rushes out of the kitchen. I clumsily wrap the apron over my school uniform which consists of a white blouse and a navy blue skirt – the only clean clothes I could find. Anyway, since the apron is at least two sizes too big it covers my outfit. It's like a wrap-around dress, which I secure at the back of my waist with its ribbons.

It's very hot in the kitchen. I open the giant fridge looking for some cold water. I have the distinct feeling of being watched.

Grand-mère wants her biscuits. Where are they?

A nasal voice behind me makes me jump. Slamming the fridge door shut, I turn around to face a pair of steely blue eyes staring at me. I feel the sweat drip down the back of my neck.

Hey, *tifi*! I'm talking to you! I said Grand-mère wants her biscuits, didn't I?

Yes, Mamzel Sophie! I was just about to get them for Madame. I'll be there in a moment. Mama, who has grown docile, is quick to intervene, in a low submissive tone she reserves for work. Her voice sounds different whenever she's around them. The words come out a little shaky. Her accent's fake. It's almost as if she's scared of that little brat of a blonde.

Mamzel Sophie gives me one hard look before traipsing out of the kitchen with her long hair trailing behind her. I wipe my sweaty hands on the apron.

What the hell do you think you're you doing? You're here not even five minutes and you're already snooping around the fridge like that! I told you not to touch anything and to stay out of trouble, didn't I? Now start polishing those dishes over there! We're using the good china today, because of Madame's guests. Mama hurriedly gathers the biscuits on to a silver plate and rushes out to the *varangue* facing the sea. *Le thé sous la varangue* is an old tradition which the family follows strictly.

She's back within a couple of minutes and starts boiling water in a big pot.

Isn't Mamzel Sophie La Reine's granddaughter?

Yes, she lives in the other part of the house with her mother, Madame Nadia. But she hangs around here after college until her mother's back from Curepipe.

I mean, isn't she the one? I prompt her.

What do you mean?

Isn't Sophie the one who kicked Marie when Marie offered to wash her hair? She spat at her and told her to wash her own smelly Afro. *Vilin tifi kreol. Lav to seve krepi santi pi.* Dirty little Creole. Go wash your own smelly Afro hair, the brat used to taunt Marie.

A shadow crossed Mama's face.

How do you know that? You were too young.

I remember Marie coming home in tears and overhearing her talking to Tantine Sybille. When Marie tried to defend herself from her vicious kicks, the brat falsely accused Marie of hitting her. Marie was dismissed on the spot. Mama tried to explain, but she ended up getting a warning from them. She couldn't afford to lose her job as well, so she shut up and accepted Marie's fate.

How dare you lay your hands on my daughter! Leave, and never come back here. *To finn konpran? Vas t'en! Oust!* Madame Nadia had spat at her. Marie was kicked out like a dog.

*Ma petite*, Sophie darling! Don't cry. *Mon ange.* My little angel. You poor thing! No one will ever hit you again. *Ma puce.* I promise you.

These damned onions are too strong. Give me that tea cloth. Mama's eyes water as she busies herself slicing chayote.

We're not here to gossip about them but to work. Now run to the potager and get me a bunch of parsley and thyme. Wash the lot in the outside sink before you come in. Oh, and some curry leaves too! Then I need you to grate the Cheddar cheese into this plate for the gratin. Chop chop. We have no time to waste. The whites like to be waited *on*, but if there's one thing they hate it's to have to wait *for* anything.

# 15

It's easier to dream than to face reality.

# 16

Mama throws the chopped chayote into the sizzling golden butter and stirs vigorously with the help of a bamboo spatula. I hand her the fresh herbs from the garden.

Did you wash that?

Of course, I lie. I secretly hope they get poisoned. Mama chops up the bundle of aromatic herbs before throwing the lot into the pan.

Now, while I finish making the *sauce blanche* for the gratin, go to the veranda and see if they're done with the tea. And be discreet!

Reluctantly, I tiptoe out of the kitchen through the back door and slide along the side of the house until I have a decent view of the veranda. I catch a whiff of Madame La Reine's cologne even before seeing her figure from the back. Madame is sitting comfortably on a planter's chair facing the sea. Mama sprinkles eau de cologne on Madame's freshly washed clothes just before ironing them. Traces of the cologne linger on Mama's coarse hands when she comes home late at night. It feels weird to have this expensive scent drift into our barracks, but it only lasts for a split second before the overbearing smell of the gutters takes over. The whiffs of another life so near and yet so far away from our own.

Once, trying to recapture that fragrance, I tried to make my own cologne by crushing citronella leaves from the vegetable patch with a freshly squeezed lemon. But the smell was too tangy, so I added a spoon of sugar in an attempt to make it sweeter. Mama caught me and told me off for wasting sugar.

47

What do you think you're doing, wasting good food like that? I work very hard to put food on the table every day. Don't you ever play with food! You hear me?

When I told her that I wasn't playing with food but trying to make perfume to get rid of the fishy smell, she emitted a bitter sound.

No amount of perfume will ever get rid of the stench of the *cité*. You're born with it. You'll carry it with you like a dark shroud enveloping you. Wherever you go. So you'd better get used to it.

*Vilin tifi kreol. To seve krepi santi pi. Vilin tifi kreol. To seve krepi santi pi.*

Dirty little Creole. Your Afro hair stinks. Dirty little Creole. Your Afro hair stinks.

*The night is still. You're exhausted from a heavy day's work serving and fawning on those spoiled brats – under the assault of the heat. But you're too afraid to close your eyes. Fear of letting down your guard. Otherwise the demons of the night might creep into you. An eerie silence descends upon Riambel. Ri-am-bel. Rire en belle. No one here's laughing. Even the dogs roaming through the night stop what they are doing as they, too, feel the presence lurking around the corner. Coming to us. Like a sudden apparition, a ghost. The shadows on the walls begin to play tricks on you. Shadows drowning souls. Playing hide-and-seek. In those little secret corners you didn't even know existed. Slipping in and out before the crack of dawn. Ghosts that carry their smells. Invasive. Cheap rum and tobacco. Stale breath. Be quiet. You're shivering like a little lamb about to get slaughtered.*

*You're scared. Tu as peur. To gagn per. Père.*

## GATO PIMA
## (CHILLI FRITTERS)

If you want fresh *gato pima* you need to soak one *gilas* of yellow split peas in a pot of water overnight. The next morning, throw away the dirty water and wash again until the water's clear. Put the pulses in a big pot of water. Add some coarse sea salt and a pinch of fresh saffron. Cover and cook until they are soft to the touch, and then drain.

On a *ros kari* or stone mortar, crush the cooked pulses with just a pinch of cumin seeds until the paste reaches a smooth consistency that's not too rough or too soft. While the paste is resting, slice a green chilli into thin strips. Chop some spring onions and a bunch of fresh coriander and add to the mixture. Sprinkle with a hint of curcuma and salt. Mix well. Take a bit of the paste in your hands and form balls the size of a small zanbalak fruit. Fry in hot oil until golden brown. Serve when it's still warm for breakfast with *pain maison* and sweet vanilla tea.

I sit on the sand and stare at the lagoon in front of me. There are a couple of fishermen at sea. The tide is low. I see Tonton Antonio, who is waving at me. He walks with difficulty. His face twitches in pain with every step he makes.

*Ki manier, Noemi?* Have you heard the news? He's panting slightly. He removes a handkerchief from his pocket and wipes the sweat off his weathered face.

*Korek Tonton? Ki news?* I don't know what he's referring to.

*Laba!* He points towards the end of the beach. There's a bunch of police near Pomponette. Getting rid of them squatters.

Why? I ask.

They're clearing the site for construction. They want to build some hotel.

Here?

Yes. *Napa res nanye.* They've used up all the beaches around the island for their five-star hotels, so now they come to exploit the wild south. For as long as I've lived here, I've never seen such police brutality. They're hitting those who resist. In front of the crying kids. They've got no shame!

When did you move to Riambel, Tonton?

A long time ago. He looks at the sea. It was during Cyclone Carol, which killed and injured so many people. We were forced to move to Riambel. I was only a child. Our huts had been completely destroyed. We had to seek shelter in government-owned schools that were made of robust concrete. Huddled together, we slept on the cold, bare floor. After the cyclone, they built some barracks near the public beach, so we stayed. Now our boy is also resting here. He's near us. Tonton nods towards the sea.

It takes me a good minute to realise that he's tilting his shiny bald head in the direction of the cemetery.

An accident on New Year's Eve, he continues. The drunk driver got away. Sebastien was riding his bicycle in the dark. Coming home from his late shift.

Where did he work?

He used to work as a janitor at Souillac hospital. His mother and I were waiting to celebrate with him, but the reckless driver got to him first. He was left to die by the side of the street. Thrown into the gutter. Instead of celebrating New Year's Day, we were organising our son's funeral. Parents shouldn't have to bury their children. It's against the laws of nature. His eyes look like salt water.

I'm sorry, Tonton. I don't know what to say, so I turn my head towards the ocean.

That was his destiny. We accepted it. He was twenty-three years old. Today he would have been forty-two. *Lavi pa fasil.* Life is hard. There's nothing we could have done. He shrugs his shoulders.

Did you ever find out who did it?

Tonton shakes his head. Some passers-by later said that it was a jeep full of drunk white kids heading towards their *kanpman*. It happened just after Souillac, near Bain des Négresses.

I ask Tonton about his childhood. He takes his time before he replies.

I've spent most of my life here, except for a few years when my mother got a job on the Du Sankray sugar estate for a *blan* as an apprentice maid. So my mother and father, me and five siblings moved there. But it was mainly my mother and us kids.

My father was in and out and did as he pleased. In the end my mother had another man.

And how was life on the estate? I ask him.

Awfully hard. His face constricts as he looks away at the glistening ocean and the sun on the horizon. I only did one week towards my Certificate of Primary Education, and then I had to stop. I didn't want to. I liked going to school. It was a place where we could escape from the estate, even if we had to walk to school barefoot and couldn't afford a pencil to write with. But I can read and write, he says proudly.

Why did you stop?

To help my mother, who couldn't manage to feed all of us on her meagre salary. They wouldn't give her a pay rise, so she asked the boss if he had a job for me. His name was Misie Brunau. He wasn't a good man. His pink face was always angry – always finding fault and calling us lazy.

He gave me the hardest job: clearing the overgrown sugar cane. I had to make a pathway through the jungle-like fields, cutting shrubs and branches until there was a clear path. The sugar cane branches sliced into my arms. I was barely eleven years old. Too small to manoeuvre the sabre correctly. Kneeling under the scorching sun, I grabbed prickly stems as close to the earth as possible and pulled and pulled using both hands. The thorns pricking my arms. Tearing them. Drawing blood that dried and stuck on my skin. But what choice did I have? That's the only job they had for me.

Tonton was silent for a while, as if recalling those long hours spent under the scorching sun, doing menial work on the estate, when all he wanted was to go to school to finish his CPE.

I used to see them. You know. The ones who stayed at school. They would pretend they didn't know me when I walked past, balancing stacks of sugar cane branches perched on my head on a *sak goni*. I looked at my feet, but deep down I knew that I was doing it so that my five siblings, who were always crying for food, wouldn't go hungry. A red rash covered their arms and feet. It was so thick that you could hardly see their skin.

How did they get the rash? I ask.

It was called the poor people's disease. It happens when you eat nothing but roots and molasses or dirty rats and mongooses caught in the fields. But I didn't steal. I worked hard. Until my hands were scarred and my back hurt.

*His gaze on you is shifty. You've seen that look too many times. His eyes watching you – always moving back and forth like a cat watching its prey. You know exactly what it means. What he's thinking. Whatever you do, you must not make eye contact. Pretend he's not there. Pretend you can't feel his hunger. His lust, as he eyes your slim wrists when you're asked to serve tea. Eyes undressing you. Perversely removing your maid's uniform that should have been a school uniform. He's an old man. As old as the sea. You're a ripe mango in his fields. For him it's only a matter of time. You slip away as quietly as possible. Like a field mouse hiding in the sugar plantation. But deep down you know your fate. The master knows his. Fat, hungry cats will catch the small field mice. Who are you but a maid in his house?*

*Patron. Patron*
*Gro Patron*
*Ena vilin lapat gro*
*Li kontan trap-trape*
*Rod-rode*
*Li krwar tou apartenir li*
*Patron. Patron*
*Gro Patron*
*Ena vilin vant ron*
*Roz kouma koson*

Master. Master
Mighty Master
With big fat paws
Always groping
Wanting more
Thinking he owns us all
Master. Master
Mighty Master
With big fat belly
Pink like piggy

# 18

The air is humid. The sky is cloudy. Tired, I sit in front of the ocean. The sea ahead of me is endless: sea as far as I can see. I want to burrow into the warm sand and sleep. So I lie on the beach as if I'm in a cot and close my eyes. My mass of hair feels like a soft pillow. The sounds of the water gently rock me to sleep. Soft murmurs of the ocean like sweet childish lullabies. A few hours later, I wake up to the scent of the lagoon at low tide. I take a deep breath, filling my lungs with the deliciously fresh morning breeze.

All alone, I witness the sun rising above the sea and I catch my breath. The faint morning light is the promise of a new world about to begin.

Above me is a lonely bird with a broken wing, struggling to fly. Flapping and fluttering in the air, it descends into the water.

The ocean and the sky blend into one. Like a scene painted with big brushstrokes of blue and grey, but the paint's still wet – waiting to dry. The colours not yet defined.

*You have to be a good girl. You'll be given a mint bonbon afterwards. To sweeten the blow. Your tender belly hurts. Soft innards. Too many mint bonbons already in your throat. Makes you feel sick. You have night cramps. Bending. Groping. Rubbing. Twisting. Pulling your tender insides. Hard. For years, you quietly wet your bed and spit slime into your pillow. The demon of the night eats you little by little. Its gluttony is endless. It gnaws like a vulture. Here. There. Everywhere. Until you're nothing. Nothing but a mere shadow.*

# 19

I like to walk barefoot on the beach. To feel the tiny particles of sand underneath my feet, gently massaging my soles. I write my name on the virgin sand.

Noemi.

No-e-mi.

No.

Emi.

Like a rebel – my name wants to protest.

To say no.

Noemi.

No-e-mi.

No.

Emi.

My name screams *no*! But no to whom? To what? I'm not really sure. The waves wash the letters away. One minute I'm there, the next minute I'm gone. Erased by the sea. Without leaving any traces behind.

My faded red dress billows in the wind. The thin straps are loose over my shoulders. It's a dress that belonged to Marie. Wearing it reminds me of her. It's comforting to have a little bit of her near me – her faded scent next to my skin. The fragrance of coconut and a hint of spices – like the aromatic cinnamon sticks she used for cooking. But slowly Marie's perfume fades away, just like my memories of her.

Sometimes, I see Marie's face shining in my dreams – like the flash of a fish under the water.

The fishermen are starting to come back from the sea, proudly displaying their catch. I pretend I don't hear their wolf whistles and carry on walking. I know they're waiting for a sign. Any sign. A look. A nod or an acknowledgement and they'll pounce.

I ignore them and stare ahead of me, listening to the soothing sounds of the waves. Whenever I stand in front of the vast ocean, I feel a little less lonely.

From a distance, I see two young tourists flying giant kites. The wind carries their laughter and snippets of their conversation. As I approach them, it becomes clear from their accents that they are not tourists but white Mauritians. Another bunch of rich white kids who think they still own us and the beach. They carry themselves differently from the rest of us. They walk with privilege and a sense of entitlement. Keeping my distance, I move a little to the side – ready to slip into the shadow.

It's as if I'm invisible. Had I been white, they would have acknowledged me. That I am sure of. But not a *tifi kreol* with a slightly squashed nose that flares, which Grand-mère used to refer to as my button nose.

One of them has an unfamiliar English accent. I hear him swear in Creole as he loses his grip and struggles trying to manoeuvre the kite. He's fighting with the strong winds, but he seems to be enjoying the challenge. It's strange to hear the white Franco-Mauritian kids speak our dialect instead of French, the noble language of their ancestry. Talking in simple Creole. *Kreol.* Our mother tongue. The language of the oppressed. For a split second our eyes meet. I suddenly see all the misery and pain of my people transfixed in those dark, greenish eyes the colour of sugar cane fields at dusk.

*You want to vanish, to sink into the twilight and quietly disappear without the world noticing.*

# 20

The sky is overcast. The air's heavy and wet. I feel its weight as I walk past headstones of different sizes and shapes, depending on the wealth and status of the deceased's family. I stop to look at some of the pictures on the tombs made of concrete or marble: Jesus crucified. An angel streaked by rain. The Virgin Mary and a few photos of the dead, once living but now fading.

The sailors' cemetery, overlooking the sea, is a mystical place for one's soul to rest. I like the ancient limewashed headstones, wind- and water-worn. The writings are difficult for me to read but I trace them with my fingers wondering what my own would look like, and imagine Mama standing by my graveside in the rain.

Right at the back is the section where the newly dead are buried. Kneeling in front of the simple stone engraved with *Marie Lasal*, I start clearing away the overgrown weeds. Once the bulk has been removed, I dig into my pocket and take out a *coquille bonheur* that I found at low tide. I place the shell on Marie's grave, on top of the pile that's already there – to bring luck in her new life. Wherever she is, I want my big sister to be happy.

A small yellow bird lands on a nearby tomb looking for something. Unable to find what it's looking for, the bird flies off into the sky in search of a kinder place where it won't have to live off scraps.

My silent tears have darkened Marie's gravestone. I am about to leave when, among the voices in my head, which torment me so often, hers starts to resonate again.

*Noemi, do not allow yourself to become a prisoner of this dump. Do not let it steal your soul like it stole mine. Run without looking back. Go! Far away from here. Never set foot in this cursed village again. Be free to live. I will only rest in peace once you've fulfilled your destiny. Do not let my grave tie you to this place. Wherever you go I will be. I promise you, my little Noemi.*

It took a while for the nightmares to disappear after Marie's death. My big sister and the only real friend I ever had. I know she was a good person who just got mixed up with the wrong lot.

After being falsely accused of hitting a white kid and dismissed from her job, it wasn't easy for her to find another. All the doors she knocked on remained closed to her. She'd been tarred. Blacklisted. There wasn't a single white family that would hire her.

A friend got her a job at a sweatshop near Chemin Grenier doing repetitive menial tasks in an airless warehouse cramped with hundreds of workers. Sweaty bodies hunched over industrial machines. Treading and sewing away. Mechanically. Routinely. For many hours a day, for almost nothing.

One morning, Marie went to work as usual only to discover that the factory had closed down overnight. Just like that. Without any warning. The doors had been bolted. Something to do with illegal workers and operating on the black market.

Unable to bear Mama's reproaches, Marie moved in with some guy she had met at work. After he left her for someone else, some 'friends' gave her a couple of 'samples' for free. A little pick-me-up, they'd say. To make the gloomy days a little sunnier. Until she became completely dependent on substances. According to some stories, she'd become a good-time girl. Mama doesn't like to talk about that phase of her older daughter's life, but she still keeps the now-faded newspaper clipping that reported Marie's death as a(nother) *fait divers*.

Marie's half-naked body was discovered by a pair of hikers near Chamarel forest – her once pretty face barely recognisable. Intoxicated. She had been abused and left to rot in the woods. Her muddy red skirt was wrapped around her head, covering her bloody face. It was a few days before her twentieth birthday.

## SALAD OURIT
## (OCTOPUS SALAD)

To make a good octopus salad that's delicious and tender, you have to make sure to boil it for at least half an hour, otherwise it'll be chewy. Wait until the octopus is as soft as butter before removing it from the heat. While your octopus is simmering in a big pot of water, cut an onion into thin slices. It's better to use purple onions instead of the bland ones, to add that extra splash of colour to the dish. Soak a bunch of watercress – which grows abundantly in the nearby rivers – for a few minutes and rinse until clean. Make sure you choose tender leaves and stalks, otherwise they taste bitter. Chop two or three tomatoes and some fresh coriander. Drain and leave to cool before slicing it. Toss all the ingredients together in a big bowl. Add a dash of oil with a squeeze of fresh lime juice and one sliced chilli. Sprinkle with some salt and pepper to taste and serve as a side dish or stuffed into a *pain maison*.

## 2 2

There's a white lady with a heart of gold who volunteers every Friday, which is my favourite day of the week. Her name's Margaret but she says we can call her Maggie. Not Mrs Maggie but just Maggie, which obviously no one ever does. Rumour has it that she used to be a hippie in England, where she met an Indo-Mauritian student on a scholarship and followed him back here after their studies.

The first time she visited our school, she introduced herself simply, without any airs whatsoever, which was surprising for a *blan*.

I came to Mauritius for a holiday some forty-odd years ago, but then I never left, she announced.

That's one hell of a long holiday, Clément quipped, without even looking up – in an obvious attempt to provoke her.

Instead of falling into his trap, she merely nodded.

Well, I guess you could say that, she said, in a tone that implied that she was not in the least offended by Clément's insolence or the way he had rolled his eyes when she entered the classroom. And then she winked at him. Even Clément was lost for words.

It was at that precise moment that I decided that I liked Mis Maggie. Not because of her white hair with streaks of gold that catch the sun, her flowery shirts or the delicious whiffs of vanilla that seem to follow her around, but because she never talks down to us, unlike most of the other teachers. Her smile feels genuine, compared to the ones you see from the replacement teachers or those who are sent to us for their training. You can always tell how they just can't wait to complete their term and bugger off to a proper school in town where the pupils are more polite and academically inclined. But not Mrs Maggie. She teaches here as a volunteer because she wants to, although no one really knows why. Even her clear brownish eyes seem to twinkle conspiratorially at us. I think the other teachers are also a little bit in awe of her, unable to understand how a foreigner has managed to gain our trust. Something they'll never be able to achieve – not in their entire lifetime.

I overheard her referring to us as *these beautiful children*. No one's ever called us that before! We mustn't write them off. Not everyone performs well in exams or under pressure. If we don't help them, then who will? she pleaded.

Another time, I heard her tell our principal that we're just children with a lot of bad luck. They ask for so little, she said.

Occasionally, Mrs Maggie gives me a pomade for the bruises I try to hide under my school blouse. She slips the small jar discreetly into my hands when no one's looking.

Try this, and if it doesn't work let me know. Her kind eyes don't judge or condemn me.

Apart from Mama's bosses I'd never been near white people before, let alone spoken to them. Mama said we shouldn't speak to the *blan* unless we're being addressed. We should always refer to them as Monsieur/Madame/Mademoiselle. And we shouldn't look directly into their eyes. It's rude.

But how come they are allowed to look straight at us? I once asked her.

It's just the way it is and always has been. Just do as I tell you.

Mama doesn't have time for all my questions.

# 2 3

For the end-of-year school excursion, instead of another picnic on the beach, Misie Ravi takes us to Domaine des Eaux to visit the famous château. We're nervous and excited at the same time. No one in our school has ever set foot in a château before – although it was our ancestors who spent their entire lives slaving away building and staffing them.

The bus drops us off on the main road. We follow a tree-lined avenue that leads to the impressive building. The property is set amid an oasis of peace and lush greenery with the odd dash of colour here and there. The roads are still damp from the tropical downpour that the plateau is famous for. The smells of wet earth and camphor fill our lungs as we climb up the ancient stone steps leading to the colonial house. We enter the building feeling a little intimidated – it is strange to use the main entrance instead of the service door reserved for the likes of us.

Misie Ravi explains that the veranda overlooking the manicured lawn was where the former owners spent most of their days. He patiently guides us around the property, as we can't afford a tour guide. We wander about the estate past the ancient stables and distillery – taking in the well-kept gardens full of exotic plants as he points at various trees and historical objects of interest.

He informs us that the château was built in 1872 and that, a few years later, it became the first property on the island to have electricity.

People from all corners of the island would travel here to catch a glimpse of the brightly lit property, he adds. It was only converted into a museum in the early 2000s, after the family moved out in the 1990s.

He glances at his notes every now and then, making sure that he doesn't miss anything important.

You mean that only one family lived here? Clément asks in disbelief.

That's right, he nods.

But Misie Ravi! That's like one thousand times bigger than our *cité*! one of the pupils quipped in awe.

That's how the colonisers used to live. Their servants slept at the back of the estate, in the shed-like barracks.

I like listening to Misie Ravi's voice. He seems so knowledgeable. He never rushes to answer each one of our questions, no matter how naïve. It's like he is seriously thinking about it, carefully choosing and measuring his words before replying.

I ask him why we don't know about the history of the people who used to work here.

That's a very good question, Noemi. Unfortunately, their lives didn't matter. They weren't important. Slaves were considered to be mere chattels.

What's a chattel? I ask him as I pick up a piece of eucalyptus wood that has fallen on the immaculate lawn. Using both hands, I bend the stick until it snaps, and inhale deeply. The strong scent is a mixture of pine and fresh mint.

He takes his time before answering.

It means property or possession, but the word 'chattel' actually comes from the word 'cattle', he finally says. Treated like animals, not human beings. Nowadays, there are more books being written about slavery to commemorate their lives and achievements, all of which are deeply rooted in the rich history of our island. Until recently, we've been exposed to versions of Mauritian history that have been whitewashed. Our history, like our bodies, is one that's been tortured over the years. It's not a coincidence that a lot of the records held during the times of colonialism have been destroyed, or that the holders claim they are lost. Some still remain in private hands, because to make this public would expose the atrocities perpetrated by the white families and their descendants. Despite what's being written in the context of the abolition of slavery, you'd be surprised that Mauritians have yet to build a museum to commemorate our former slaves.

Why haven't they? I ask.

He scratches his beard, searching for his words. Well, for lack of funding, they say. It's not that black and white, apparently. Practically all of the private companies approached have benefited from the exploitation of slaves. Most of these cartels have been built on sugar wealth, and their owners are reluctant to donate to this cause. Mauritians don't like to be reminded of the racial imbalance mothered by our colonial legacy. Or to have to face a violent past that's still very much embedded in our modern society. It makes them uncomfortable.

I stop to admire an assortment of wild orchids growing precariously on the bark of a tree, and it strikes me how their scarlet colour bleeds into the rest of the delicate white flower.

But it's been a while since they abolished slavery, I add.

Yes, you're right, Noemi. But attitudes don't change that easily here. There's still a very long way to go. But we'll continue fighting for that museum, he sighs, before glancing at his watch. Oh, look at the time! he exclaims. We'd better make a move if we want to catch the last bus to the south. Let's all meet in front of the building in fifteen minutes, he shouts at the groups of pupils scattered about the lawn.

*Sometimes, when the day wanes, you hear the piercing cries of the fugitive slaves, the lashings of the whips and babies weeping.*

# 2 4

I follow a couple of girls into the small boutique selling gifts and souvenirs, although it's clear that we can't possibly afford anything. The trinkets, which are priced in euros, are squarely aimed at tourists. The shop assistant keeps a careful eye on our every move.

Can I help you, she asks haughtily, with an expression of disdain on her heavily made-up face.

*Nou pe nek gete.* We're just looking.

Please don't touch anything! You'll have to pay for any damage, she warns us.

We quietly ignore her. As we leave the gift shop feeling deflated, I overhear her talking to her colleague, who has a red bindi on her forehead. The woman looks at us as if she's smelled something bad – like a dead rat, or worse.

*Bann ti nasion sorti site. Bizin bien vey zot. Zot ena lame long.* Creole girls from slums. We need to keep a close watch over them. They are prone to stealing.

I turn around to have one last look at the Château du Domaine des Eaux. I feel its ugly past weighing on my bony shoulders, pressing down on me. I begin to see it in a different light – one that's much darker than the embellished stories sold to gullible tourists. I wonder if some of my great-great-grandparents worked here. What traces of their lives remain apart from this building and my own existence? Weren't their lives and souls stolen to build this grand colonial place? *Bann voler.* And they call *us* thieves.

# 2 5

The following afternoon, I join Mama after school. Instead of helping her in the kitchen, she says I should clean the living room. I gingerly enter the big salon full of antique furniture that's been in the De Grandbourg family for generations. I don't like those stern faces with their faux-aristocratic noses looking down from the portraits hanging in heavy gilt frames. Their blue eyes are full of disdain for the likes of me. I hurriedly dust the furniture, trying to avoid their white gaze.

The other side of the wall is lined with sketches and paintings of colourful dodos. The childlike drawings remind me of the ones I've seen on postcards. I lean closer to a frame. Bending my head a little, I read the inscription *Chazal*, painted in loopy letters on the right-hand corner. The surname sounds familiar. It occurs to me that I am staring at the original work of the Franco-Mauritian artist we are learning about in class: Malcolm de Chazal.

We recently worked on a school project to create a piece of art inspired by local artists. My attempt at painting a vivid landscape of the sea was so clumsy, with blobs of blue scattered here and there, that even the teacher couldn't find a kind word to say about it. After a cursory glance at my finished work, she leaned over Nathalie's desk to admire her painting of *sega* dancers.

Noemi, could you please try and make an effort next time! she spat out, before moving on to congratulate Nathalie. Good work, Nathalie – what a clever use of the palette!

The teacher's voice echoes in my head.

When I turn around, I meet with a pair of lazy green eyes. I look down and unconsciously straighten my apron before dashing out of the room towards the kitchen, where Mama's awaiting me with hundreds of tasks.

*Excusez-moi! Vous avez oublié ceci!* he says with a slight accent, before handing me my dusting cloth. My piece of rag. I had left it on the stained teapoy made of shiny ebony.

*Merci, Monsieur,* I murmur back.

Do you like that painting? his voice drawls, just as another figure enters the room.

*Mais qu'est ce qui t'arrives? Tu parles aux domestiques maintenant?* Mademoiselle Sophie quips flippantly.

Sophie, you can't say things like that! Times have changed, you know! he whispers audibly, looking mildly shocked.

Oh, *mon pauvre* Alexandre! Just because you've been living in Australia all these years, you seem to have forgotten that this is Mauritius! *Ça ne se fait pas,* OK? We don't talk to servants. Come on. Let's go outside for some fresh air. *Ça pue le nègre ici.* It stinks of negroes in here, she says, scrunching up her freckled nose.

My hands begin to shake uncontrollably. I look down at my bare feet, struggling to fight the tears as I swallow salt. I feel his piercing green eyes still on me – I'm not sure if I catch a glimpse of pity or something else in his catlike eyes.

# 26

Misie Ravi must have said something to Mrs Maggie about my interest in the history of slaves in Mauritius. On Friday, she strides into the classroom brandishing a book like a trophy.

I heard that you'd like to know more about the bitter legacy of slavery in the colonies.

I nod shyly, not wanting to be the centre of attention.

As you know, I'm an activist fighting for the rights of the people, says Mrs Maggie. She tells us about institutionalised oppression and resisting patriarchy with her blonde hippie plaits wrapped around her head like an angel.

History's a very interesting word – told by men. History literally means *his story*. Women have been hidden from history, and we need to bring their stories into the light. It's important to remember the past, and to honour the lives of those women who were even less visible. They deserve to be widely known.

For centuries, we've been told history from the perspective of the white man. But what about the perspective of the enslaved? Black lives don't matter. Watered down. Airbrushed out of history.

That's the danger of a single story. What about the suffering of the enslaved black women? What do we know about them? The voice of the oppressed. Remember the other side of the story.

Don't just talk about *history* but also about *herstory*. Her. Story.

Learning about your past will help you shape your identity and resist the same fate. Things can change. Think about anti-apartheid Africa and the new wave of resistance led by Nelson Mandela, who – only a couple of decades ago – became the first black president of South Africa. Who would have thought? she asks.

We quietly listen to her. A sea of shiny brown faces hanging on to her words. I notice that even Clément's paying attention.

In the next class, I'd like to talk to you about the exile of the Chagossian population, who were forced to leave Chagos, their home, their lives, to live here – in cockroach-infested barracks.

I want to put into perspective the role played by women, in particular Chagossian women, in keeping this struggle alive. The arrest and trial of eight women following street demonstrations in the arteries of Port Louis. These women were leading a hunger strike in the Jardin de la Compagnie when the riot police attacked them. A battle ensued. After a number of court hearings, with riot police bringing fierce dogs, to keep order they said, the women, including Charlesia Alexis and Lindsey Collen, were all found

Not.

Guilty.

They were not causing a disturbance or being disorderly.
They.
Were.
Merely.
Speaking.
The.
Truth.

And the Mauritian government finally acted. This one event – the arrests around the hunger strike – represents the fight, led by women from the very beginning, that continues today.

It's long and arduous struggles that bring change and not, as old-fashioned historians still pretend, a matter of prime ministers and governments. No. It is thinking people who work out collectively how to act. We should remind ourselves of this. She bangs her fist on the desk for emphasis.

I like listening to Mrs Maggie and hearing the passion in her voice. The way she makes us question things and exhorts us not simply to believe whatever nonsense we're told.

I've always wondered why there isn't any mention of people like me in textbooks. The history we are taught is not about anyone in my family. Even in our meagre school library, the books imported from Europe are full of foreign faces having adventures in faraway places. I never see myself in those stories. Because people like me aren't good enough to be in books. Our lives are not worth writing about.

*The past is your present, but don't let the past be your future.*

# 2 7

Hurry up and polish these champagne flutes! Mama barks at me.

I pick up a heavy glass and polish it until it shines.

Who's the one with the green eyes? I ask.

That's Monsieur Alexandre. Madame's grandson. He only arrived a couple of days ago. He's here for the summer.

I hold the flute up and admire how it catches the light.

Why do you ask? Mama carefully places an assortment of petits fours on a silver étagère.

He seems different. Not like the rest of them.

They're all the same, that lot. Hurry up, girl! No time to chit-chat. They'll be here in no time to check on us.

The caterers will be here any minute! Madame's voice shrills from the living room.

Mama mutters something under her breath while Garson, the gardener, and I cluster together like nervous animals.

# 2 8

Carefully, I help Mama place the exquisite-looking *napolit-aines* on a silver platter. They've been specially ordered for the party from the posh bakery in Curepipe, the one next to the church, Mama tells me.

Each one of them has been coated with pink icing that looks and smells so good that I feel myself drooling. I imagine how they must taste: moist and crumbly, oozing with guava jam. But servants are not allowed to touch the food reserved for the VIP guests who've driven from all around the island to celebrate this big event. Madame has even flown in a few members of her family from abroad. Today, she looks like a real queen, in her coral outfit with diamonds sparkling from her earlobes. Mama says that a minister will also be here this evening.

It's Sir Roger, she whispers importantly. The one who's always on TV. I caught sight of his chauffeur and bodyguard earlier. He's a bit of a looker, that one, she giggles coyly.

All evening, we hear live music from the band playing on the veranda. The laughter of the guests reaches us in the kitchen, where the heat is unbearable. Using my tea towel, I shoo away the insects trilling in from outside.

La Reine looks very pleased with herself. The guests are having a lot of fun, Mama says. All these months of planning and preparing have paid off.

From the kitchen window, I admire the palm trees decorated with colourful paper lanterns which sway in the sea breeze. Long dining tables covered with vases full of bird of paradise flowers have been set up right next to the beach. Garson spent the whole day digging holes for the torches along the tree-flanked entrance. There are hundreds of beautiful small lights scattered around the garden and swimming pool, making the property look magical under the stars. Like something straight out of a fairy tale. Not that I would know much about fairy tales.

A few waiters are hovering around ready to fawn upon the rosy-cheeked guests, who look resplendent in their evening outfits. Apart from the servants and the caterers there isn't a single brown or dark-skinned Mauritian among those present.

After hours on my feet, washing hundreds of dirty dishes in the stuffy kitchen, my calves begin to hurt. My hands are sore and my belly's rumbling. I can't remember the last time I ate.

When Mama brings in another tray of dirty dishes, I find a partly eaten *napolitaine* on the side of a plate, half-covered by a serviette. I pop it into my mouth. It tastes even better than I thought it would. I go through the leftovers and eat with my hands – wolfing down the discarded scraps.

There's some leftover champagne at the bottom of a crystal flute. The golden liquid still looks sparkly. Making sure I'm out of Mama's sight, I don't even bother wiping the coat of red lipstick off the rim before taking a sip. I let the tiny bubbles linger on my tongue before they reach the back of my throat. Feeling excited and grown-up, I finish the rest of the sparkling drink before soaping the glass in hot water. For the rest of the evening I carry the deliciousness inside me – a rich secret to savour.

Mama says I should go back home.

That's enough for one day. Leave your apron here and go. I'll stay a bit longer with Garson and clean up. The caterers will also help. And don't forget that we'll have to get up extra early tomorrow to tidy up the rest. Try and get some sleep. Tomorrow's going to be a long day! She sighs into the night.

It's way past midnight when I finally leave the De Grandbourgs' residence. I only have to cross the street to our place, but tonight I decide to take the longer route via the beach.

The lanterns dangling from bamboo sticks scattered on the beach and the full moon are enough to light up my path.

Having stood for several hours, it feels good to sit down on the cool sand for a few minutes, listening to the gentle sounds of the waves. Every now and then, the sea breeze carries a soft melody to my ears. The band is playing an old French song I've often heard on the radio. I try to make out the words.

*Ce soir j'ai envie*
*De déposer mon tablier*
*De me faire belle pour toi…*
*Emmène-moi danser ce soir*
*Joue contre joue*
*Et serrés dans le noir*
*Fais-moi la cour comme aux premiers instants*
*Comme cette nuit où tu as pris mes dix-sept ans*
*Emmène-moi danser ce soir*

*Flirtons ensemble*
*Enlacés dans le noir…*

This evening I want to shed my apron
And make myself pretty for you…
Take me dancing tonight
Let's embrace in the dark
Cheek to cheek
Woo me like you did the first time
When I was only seventeen…

# 30

There are shadows dancing cheek to cheek on the beach. A couple of party guests are smoking. They share a joke and their drunken laughter fills the air. I recognise one of them as Madame's grandson from Australia. Since I am sitting in the dark, next to a bush, no one sees me, so I ignore them and continue scrutinising the blackness of the sea. I look up and see bats whirling through the night looking for food.

A few minutes later, someone walks towards the beach in my direction. Not wanting to bring any attention to myself, I crouch a little. Still as a mouse, I wait for them to go away.

I recognise Monsieur Alexandre's silhouette in the dark as he lies back on the sand. He lights up a cigarette and breathes a long thin trail of smoke into the night.

I discreetly get up to leave, but he notices me.

Hey!

I walk away, pretending I haven't heard him.

Hey! *Bonsoir!* he calls again.

I return his greeting and continue walking towards the street as fast as possible.

Wait! Don't go.

Before I know it, he's by my side.

I recognise you! You work for my grandma.

He speaks Creole with an accent.

Nervous, I nod in the dark.

I wanted to apologise for what my cousin Sophie said. She's still very immature and has a lot of growing up to do.

I don't know what to say. No one in his family has ever spoken to me except to give orders, let alone to apologise. It's just too much for me to take in. I continue walking, feeling uneasy in his presence. I assume he will go away, but he follows me as if he's expecting an answer.

It's fine, I finally say, hoping that he'll now leave me alone, but he continues walking beside me.

I'm Alexandre, by the way.

I don't say anything.

What's your name? His body sways a little in the sand.

Noemi, I murmur.

Sorry, I didn't catch that?

Noemi, I say, louder this time.

I'll walk you back home, Noemi. He is slurring a little.

That really won't be necessary, Monsieur. I just have to cross the road.

Instead of letting me go, he starts telling me that he's already tired of being with his family and their ways of thinking.

*Ekoute*, he says, as if he has just had a brilliant idea. I have university friends from Australia visiting the island for the Christmas holidays. They'll be driving down south tomorrow. We're going to be hanging around on the beach the next few days. *Nou pou kas enn ti poz lor laplaz.* Do drop by if you're around. He beams in the dark.

Surely he must be joking! He's definitely drunk and doesn't know what the hell he's saying.

*Bonne nuit, Noemi!* he says as I'm about to enter the *cité*, a world away from the glittery one I've just been in. A neighbourhood that reeks of beer cans and salted fish. The underbelly of Riambel and its ghosts that lurk in the shadows.

A completely different world.

As different as night and day.

One that has nothing to do with his.

## 3 1

There is sweetness in the air. Bright stars twinkle in a pair of eyes. But whose eyes: those of Monsieur, or yours?

## SATINI POMDAMOUR
## (TOMATO CHUTNEY)

To make a good *satini pomdamour* you first have to roast a few tomatoes directly on an open fire until they are slightly charred. Remove from the heat and let the slightly burnt tomatoes cool before peeling off their skins. Mash the tomatoes into a pulp. Fry one chopped onion and some crushed garlic in a little bit of oil until golden. Add a sliced green chilli and a pinch of sea salt. Throw in some chopped coriander leaves. Pour this piping-hot oil mixture over your tomato paste. Mix well. Serve with curry or a simple bouillon and rice.

# 3 2

At night, I read photocopied excerpts from the book that Mrs Maggie brought into school. I can hear her clear words resonate in my head.

The white man's gaze.

Enslaved women weren't just passive victims. They joined the rebellion. Fighting alongside men.

Don't believe everything you're told to believe.

Patriarchy wants to control you.

Ask questions and think for yourself.

Don't fall into their trap.

They'll.

Just.

Screw.

You.

# 33

On Sunday, we get dressed for morning mass. The church is a relatively large one, made of old, dark stones, just off the coastal road. It's not a long walk from the *cité*, but the sun beats down on us. My armpits feel sticky after a few steps under the assault of the heat. I try to find shade whenever I can, if only for a brief moment. On our way, we pass a few street merchants heading for the public beach. Sunday is by far their busiest day of the week.

A few minutes later we reach the congregation, wearing their Sunday best. Greetings and kisses are exchanged under the big flame tree that shelters us from the scorching sun. It is like a giant red umbrella over a blanket of scarlet flowers that have fallen on the cobbled street, like an offering from the blue sky. I go out of my way to avoid squashing them with my Bata sandals. The others don't seem to care. I watch, sadly, as the delicate petals are stamped upon by a multitude of feet.

On the other side of the church, there's another cluster of families also clad in their Sunday best – waving at each other as they park their flashy vehicles under the shade of the giant badamier. They kiss each other's rosy cheeks, still cool from their air-conditioned cars, and exchange pleasantries in French.

*Quel plaisir de vous voir!*

*Mais vous êtes ravissante!*

*Ah, quel beau sac à main!*

Hurry up, girl, says Mama, as she rushes inside the church to find a good spot before they are all taken.

The inside of the ancient church is always refreshingly cool after our walk under the burning sun. We're about to enter the building when we see a Franco-Mauritian family hovering nearby. Although we are a few steps ahead of them, Mama and I immediately step aside to let them through first, as is expected of us. They head straight for the front pews nearest to the altar, which are reserved for the whites, while we loiter towards the rear. A few seconds too late, we watch the last seats in the back row being taken by a family with two toddlers bouncing on a harassed-looking mother.

From the corner of my eye, I see the De Grandbourg family already seated – right next to God, obviously. And every week, it's the same routine. We pretend not to know each other and look the other way.

Never mind, whispers Mama. We remain standing throughout the entire service, despite the vacant places in front with the *blan*, who would never accept one of us siting anywhere near them. *Ça ne se fait pas!* Even after mass we wait patiently for them to leave the church first.

All our lives we've walked around them. On silent tiptoes. Reverently. Serving them. Waiting on them. We're taught never to inconvenience them. They walk differently – with privilege. A sense of entitlement only reserved for the whites.

Should they happen to walk in our direction, we quickly step back and let them go first. If we're waiting in a queue, they won't stand in line like the rest of us. *Certainement pas!* They'll always be served first.

After saying goodbye to our acquaintances, we cross the street and head towards the beach. Mama and I treat ourselves to a roti from the Muslim lady who has a makeshift kitchen under the almond tree facing the sea. The lady pulls her saree around her and ties the *horni* around her pot belly.

As the flat tawa is heating over the naked gas fire, she tears a piece from her dough and shapes it into a little ball before rolling it out into a paper-thin circle. While the roti is cooking on the hot tawa, she uses a cloth to dab some oil on it before flipping it over for the other side to cook for a few more seconds. Using her fingers, she rotates the edges until the roti rises into a puff – the consistency perfectly light and fluffy, as it should be.

We eat our piping-hot roti hungrily, as the spicy butter bean sauce dribbles down our hands. After using the paper wrapping to wipe them clean, we wash our meal down with a cold glass of creamy *alouda*. I greedily gulp the pink drink in one go.

This is the best part of Sunday. Whenever Mama's feeling particularly generous, we buy two packets of fresh green mango salad with juicy pineapple slices marinated in crushed red chillies and sweet tamarind sauce, which we save for later.

With our bellies satisfied, we head back home, where Mama removes her Sunday outfit and washes off the make-up that's melting down her face. I know that she won't be receiving any visitors today, because she puts on her old jersey house dress that's frayed along the edges. She turns on the TV, happy to vegetate in front of her favourite soap operas for the next few hours. Because Mama's usually more relaxed on Sundays than workdays, she'll let me roam about on my own to explore the quiet beaches near the sailors' cemetery, after telling me to stay out of trouble.

# BOUILLON
## (BROTH)

When you cook rice, make sure you don't throw away the water it's cooked in. Save the starch water and use it for a good bouillon which is easy to make with whatever greens you have at hand.

In a hot *karay*, add crushed ginger and garlic paste and one chopped onion. Let the mixture sizzle in a little bit of oil until golden brown. Pour in the leftover starch water and a bunch of watercress. Stir the broth for a couple of minutes until the leaves are tender and remove from heat. Add salt and pepper to taste.

You can use any other leafy vegetables, like moringa leaves or bred malbar, which grow wild on the plantations. You can also drop in some chunks of fried fish. The soft pieces will add a sea-salty flavour to the tasty vegetable broth.

Serve with rice accompanied by *rougay* and a spicy *zasar bilinbi*. There's nothing like a good bouillon with a salted fish *rougay* to satisfy your belly after a hard day's work.

*Petite négresse.*
*Little temptress.*
*You're a tease.*
*A seductress.*

# 3 4

We're an odd group, drinking and smoking pot around a campfire on the beach. Someone says, Let's lace it with something stronger. A small packet materialises out of nowhere. Boy, this is good shit, someone else announces a few minutes later. It hurts. It's sweet. It's bitter. It's liberating. My head begins to spin. And then I float, no longer scared of the secrets of the night. I close my eyes and see the stars above. A whole new galaxy twinkling and shining in the darkness. Was it always there? I can't remember it being so bright. We soar and we swoop. I feel my spirit fly high like those colourful kites across the lagoon – above the sugar cane fields towards the Le Morne mountain. Deliciously high. We dance sega around the fire. Letting our bodies move gracefully to the rhythm of the *ravann*. Swaying our hips. Like the former slaves used to. For a brief moment, I am happy and free. Or at least I think I am. Your rebellious eyes search mine. At night, your green eyes are the shade of tangling sea grass in the ocean, translucent seaweed meeting smouldering black coal.

Who wants to go for a midnight swim? People start to drift until we're alone, sitting next to each other with nothing but a burning fire between our bodies.

# 35

I see you across the bonfire. Your face is as dark and smooth as molten chocolate. Soft and glowing in the flames. It's an odd group, but I see you wandering on the beach, a lost soul. I ask you to join us. Me? *Mwa, Monsieur Alexandre?* you ask, with big eyes as deep as the ocean. You hesitate at first, but then you notice a guy with blonde Rasta hair that looks like dry hay and you decide to stay. The others look uncomfortable, but who are they to tell me who to invite? And then a bottle of rum is passed around and they quickly forget your presence in the shadows. They are easily distracted, that lot. I hand you a plastic cup and fill it up. You take a sip and make a grimace. Is it too strong? You nod. I add some Coke and drop a couple of ice cubes and a slice of lime from the cooler into it. Better? You whisper, Yes, thank you, Monsieur Alexandre. You sit cross-legged a little apart from the circle, not sure if you should really be here with us. It's clear that you're not used to it. You look around as if you can't believe you've been invited to sit with us. In this secluded ring where you don't belong. Hovering on the edge. Bordering the periphery, you sit more outside the circle than in. You gulp your drink to hide your uneasiness. A few minutes later, I roll a joint and you catch my eyes from across the flames. Your dark eyes lock with mine as I pass you the joint. Our hands meet briefly. Delicately, you place it between your moist lips and take small puffs, as if unsure what to do. You relax a little – your shoulders are less tense. You tilt your head and take in the music. Slowly, you begin to let go, moving your body gently to the sounds of the beat. I watch you as the smoke escapes your glistening lips – your mouth is half-open. I want to touch your smooth face. To open your full lips with my fingers and drown myself completely in you. Like a vessel lost at sea, I'm sinking. Pulled adrift by the forces of the waves. Deep into the dark underbelly of a mysterious ocean full of secrets.

# 36

It's the alcohol. The drugs. The sky and the stars. It's the bonfire on the empty beach at night. It's the warm sand we're sitting on. The motion of the sea and the full moon above us. You take my face into your delicate ivory hands. Softly. Your mouth meets my quivering lips. I shiver. I'm nervous. I'm cold. I'm hot. I'm burning. I'm wet. There's fire all around us. We're all lips and hands. Tracing maps – discovering lost continents with our tongues. Navigating new territories. North. South. East. West. Flames in our mouths. A fusion of colours. A confluence of desires. Opening. Hot fire. Like lava. Gurgling and boiling. About to erupt. Flooding. Melting all over you. You kneel on the soft bed of sand – your pale forehead against mine. You pray. So hard – like you've never prayed before. The wind catches your prayer. You chant over and over, like a mantra, *Noemi!* No. Emi. Don't stop. Yes. Emi. Yes. Don't stop.

*Noemi! What are you doing to me.*

*Noemi.*

*Tell me.*

*What have you done to me?*

Limp, you whisper into the silence of the night.

# 3 7

Did you say *petite négresse* or you little temptress?
I wish I could remember.

# 38

When blind people dream – can they see colours?

*Dans mon rêve*
*J'embrasse tes lèvres*
*Douces comme un jour d'été qui se lève*

In my dreams
I kiss your lips
As sweet as the dawn of a summer's day

# 39

I don't know what's happening to me. I have never experienced anything like this before. It's like everything's different, but at the same time nothing's really changed. I am just the same, aren't I? But why I am seeing things differently? When I look at the night sky from my small window, the stars twinkling from above seem to shine brighter than before.

And when I'm with him, it's like the tide is turning. I forget who I am and where I'm from. Nothing matters any more.

# 40

After a restless night, I wake up to a timid dawn. I sneak out and head towards the ocean. The wind no longer blows against me, lifting me forwards as if I have little springs in my steps. My shoulders no longer feel heavy and hunched. I walk towards the sea feeling taller, no longer scared of its infinity. A welcoming blanket of sapphire blue. The ocean whispers to me. Luring me. As if in a trance, I tear off all my clothes and surrender myself completely to the water. I dive head first into a sea full of promise. My arms and legs spread like a starfish. Softly, the morning waves caress me. I let myself go. Submerged by the sea. I close my eyes and forget about the world – carried away by the water gently lapping between my legs. Licking my budding breasts. Tenderly. Entering me. I am wet. I am drifting. Deliciously floating. In a pool of dreams.

## 41

For him I want to be like the sea. Mesmerisingly beautiful. Fluid. Wild. Mysterious and free.

# 42

I can't sleep. The chirping of the bulbuls wakes me up. Lingering in bed, I enjoy the silence of the house and the sound of the nearby ocean. The fishermen are back from the sea. They always try their luck with the villagers first, before heading to the market. As Mama rarely buys from them, they don't linger outside our gate advertising their wares for too long.

You're going to be late for school!

All I can think of is Alexandre's hands and mouth on me, and the thought makes me giddy with excitement.

Noemi! Get up, Mama says, interrupting my daydream.

I'm already up! I shout back. I can hear Mama shuffling around in the room next door.

Can you prepare tea? I have to go early today.

I reluctantly get up and venture into the kitchen area. The *deksi* is still dirty from yesterday, so I give it a quick rinse before filling it with just enough water for two cups.

While the water's boiling I make my bed – straightening the cotton sheets and tucking the edges neatly in like Grand-mère taught me to do. When the water starts to hum, I throw two teaspoons of vanilla-flavoured tea leaves and a piece of cinnamon stick into the pan. Then I add a cardamom pod and let the tea brew. Powdered milk is used sparingly in our household, so I only add a sprinkling of it, together with a teaspoon of unrefined sugar which Mama buys cheaply in bulk. Most people prefer refined sugar, but I prefer the rawness of brown sugar with a hint of molasses – much tastier than plain white sugar.

With the help of a steel strainer, I pour the fragrant tea into two cups and lightly butter a piece of bread.

It's ready, I shout out to Mama, who is trying to get her mass of hair to fit neatly into a bandana. The quicker she has her breakfast of *dite dipin diber*, the quicker Mama will be out of the house and I can get ready in peace.

I want to look good today. Alexandre asked me to meet him after school. I don't want Mama to see me put make-up on.

She'd tell me off. Mascara for school? *Arek fer to alert!*

Yesterday, I sneaked into La Balance after school and bought a new lipstick from the Indian hairdresser. It wasn't cheap, but the lady said it's top-notch. Apparently all the Bollywood lookalikes are wearing it.

I want to please Alexandre. I can't wait to see his green eyes on me – his hands hastily removing my school uniform. Hungrily. Soft hands that have never known a hard day's work – devoid of the calluses we're plagued with. Beautiful ivory hands playing me over and over like a piano – making sweet music.

# 43

I'm busy humming away while slicing onions when Mama barges into the kitchen, out of breath.

Quick, Noemi! Leave what you're doing and help me set all this up.

I wipe my teary eyes using the end of my apron.

Madame tells me they've just received a guest. An unexpected visit, and you know what they're like! They like to impress visitors. So we'll now have to change the tea china and use the gold-plated one they reserve only for guests!

I pat my hands dry, drop the tea towel and obediently follow Mama to the terrace, wondering who this special guest could be whose visit is causing such a commotion. Probably some fusty relative visiting from the other side of the island. After being stuck in a stuffy kitchen, I welcome the sea breeze on my face, which is glistening with sweat.

Mama and I reset the tables as quickly as we can. There are only a few minutes left before teatime and the De Grandbourg clan will be expecting everything to be ready. Mama hands me a pair of secateurs and asks me to put some fresh flowers in the porcelain vase. I cut a few frangipani blossoms and arrange the little bouquet nicely in the middle of the table.

We're so late. They'll be here any minute now. Mama begins to panic as we hear distant laughter and approaching footsteps.

I hate to see her like that, so I help her as best I can.

Oh, I forgot the milk. Here! She hands me the milk jug.

Go get some from the fridge. It's in the bottom drawer. And hurry up! They're coming.

By the time I've gone to the kitchen to locate the milk, most of the De Grandbourg congregation is already seated and chatting nonchalantly about their sea excursion.

We caught a *mari gro* marlin! You should have seen the size of it! one of the rich kids is bragging.

You might be good at catching fish, but when it comes to hunting I'm the best deer hunter in the south. Those little animals stand no chance. I can't wait for the hunting season to commence. My guns are all polished and ready to start the kill, boasts another cousin in a nasal voice. His face is as pasty as a white loaf of bread.

Oh, enough showing off, you two! Here come the groom and bride-to-be! announces Sophie, just as the doors open to reveal Alexandre, who's smiling adoringly at a tall blonde girl with the clearest blue eyes I've ever seen.

Groom and bride-to-be? I feel my stomach tighten as I stay glued to the spot watching the couple enter, hand in hand.

Grand-mère, I would like you to meet Rachel, my fiancée, who has flown in for a surprise visit.

*Bienvenue, ma chère!* Welcome, my dear! Just as Madame flashes one of her rare smiles, the jug I have been holding slips from my sweaty hands and lands with a crash on the tiles.

My face is hot and flustered as all eyes are on me.

Mama's looking at me very crossly from the other side of the room, where she's nervously pouring tea into dainty white cups.

I mumble an awkward apology.

You clumsy girl! That Limoges set has been in my family for generations! Madame shrieks in horror.

*Mais quelle incapable!* Useless maid! she snaps, looking at the shattered pieces on the ancient black and white tiles. Her face is a fist.

*Je suis vraiment désolée, Madame.*

*Quel gâchis!* Don't just stand there, *tifi!* Go get a mop and clean this mess up.

I run out of the room wiping hot tears with the end of my apron.

When I come back with a dustpan and a mop, they've already moved on. Mama has brought another supply of fresh milk for their tea. I'm acutely aware of Alexandre's green eyes on me as I kneel down to pick up the shattered pieces one by one.

I don't look up when he pops open the champagne.

*Félicitations!*

Cheers.

*Santé.*

To the happy couple.

Ignoring the sounds of clinking glasses, I mop the floor until it gleams. The ancient black and white flagstones are no longer shrouded by a cloud of milk but spotlessly clean. For the first time, I notice how each black tile is clearly separate from the dazzling white ones that catch the afternoon sun.

There's.

No point.

In crying.

Over spilled milk.

Mama tells me afterwards.

*Je suis l'ombre. Je suis la fille des écumes abandonnée et rejetée sur une plage déserte.*

I am the shadow. I am the daughter of waves, abandoned and rejected on an empty beach.

*Oh belle nuit*
*Sur cette falaise où je suis*
*Pour me donner des ailes*
*les étoiles ont crié!*
*D'où viennent ces étincelles,*
*Cet appel et ce cri?*
*Ni aigle, ni hirondelle*
*Mais la douleur d'un oubli*
*Tombée des nuages*
*Frêle esquive contre les rafales*
*Ce corps fait naufrage…*

Oh, sweet night
The stars cried out
To give me wings
On this cliff where I stand!
Where did these glimmers,
This call and cry, come from?
Neither eagle, nor swallow,
But the pain of a forgetting
Fallen from the clouds.
Shaky push against the gusts
This body is shipwrecked…

# 44

I watch the waves break at my feet. My body staggers as the wind blows against me. The long shoreline stretches endlessly, as far as I can see. An empty bed of sand. I pick up a broken shell from a pile of dead coral washed up on the shore. I dig a ditch with my foot like a shallow grave and bury it in the sand.

A graveyard of broken dreams.

# 45

I still smell the sea in his hair, on his golden skin as smooth as a pebble from La Rivière des Galets.

# 46

It's their last evening in Mauritius. They are flying back first thing in the morning. Mama tells me that Madame is planning an intimate farewell dinner, during which she will hand over a piece of jewellery to Rachel. As an engagement gift, to welcome her into their clan.

It's a family tradition, says Mama, who's getting ready for her evening shift. She dabs a little red gloss on her full lips and smacks them in front of the mirror.

I told Mama I wasn't feeling well and couldn't help serve dinner that evening, so I stayed in the kitchen all afternoon for the preparations and then left their residence as soon as I could.

Don't worry. I'll save you some leftover foie gras, Mama says, trying to comfort me.

As if I care! I don't give a damn about their foie gras!

But after work, I discreetly follow the couple on the beach. From a distance, I watch how Alexandre holds Rachel's hand and smiles at her tenderly. Together, they walk into the horizon. I notice how his golden skin catches the light and the sun kisses his auburn hair. He is the sun. Awash with longing, I want him to look at me the way he looks at her. For him to caress my face with his ivory hands. But I know he will never do that again. I turn around and stomp back to the *cité*, giving a hard kick to a dirty beer can that has been tossed on to the pure white sand.

At night, I weep into my pillow.

I cry for my grandmother. For my mother and for my sister. For what we've been. For what I am. And for what we'll always be.

*petite esclavée que je suis*

# 47

Last night I had a strange dream. I was standing on a bridge admiring a picturesque scene on the side where I didn't belong. I stood on the periphery, looking from a distance. Floating between belonging and not belonging, I was refusing to cross it, for fear of what would happen if I reached the other side.

Somehow, drawn in by some invisible force, I managed to cross the bridge and become part of the enchanting scenery for a fleeting moment, before running back to my own side. The wooden bridge I had been balancing on was dangerously fragile, threatening to collapse at any time, leaving behind nothing but a few shattered pieces of broken wood. And some shreds of distant memories of what it was like being on the other side. Of what could have been. In a place where I'll never belong.

Tous les jours
Me hante ce chagrin d'amour
Pour vous, rien de plus banal
Dans votre vie privilégiée règne le sang ancestral

Hélas, mon petit cœur brisé
En a pleuré des flots de larmes
Si seulement vous aviez pu
Mais vous n'avez pas voulu

Je l'ai vite compris, petite fille esclavée que je suis
Descendante des gens de servitude et négritude
Rien à marquer à la pierre blanche
Une peau basanée, beaucoup trop brune

Qui ne devait surtout pas vous salir
Dans mes tristes souvenirs
Il ne reste qu'un goût doux-amer
Comme le café noir encré dans ma chair

Adieu, horreurs
Adieu, ô douleur je l'espère
Adieu, cœur saignant qui pleure
Adieu, mon seigneur!

Every day
This heartache haunts me,
It's for you, pure and simple
You got everything in that life old blood gave you

Well, my little broken heart
It's cried a river
If only you could have
But you wouldn't

I saw it plenty quick, I'm a little slave girl after all
My mothers were servants, my mothers were negroes
Nothing should stain that white stone
Darky ebony skin that's too brown

Which absolutely mustn't dirty you
All my memories are sad, in them
All that's left is bittersweetness
Like the ink-black coffee that's in my flesh

Farewell, to horrors
Farewell, to pain, I hope
Farewell, my bleeding heart, which sobs
Farewell, my lord!

# 48

Just because I'm less fortunate than you doesn't make me unworthy of your respect.

# 49

I try to read, but I can't concentrate. The words dance in front of me, mocking me. Laughing at me. Taunting me.

I throw the book across the room. Then I pick it up and smooth out the pages. I read a line over and over before staring blankly at the page. My mind keeps drifting. The words no longer make any sense.

Never before have Robert-Edward Hart's odes to the sea caused me so much pain and distress.

Looking out of the window, listening to the murmurs of the sea and the wind. Time has slowed down, the hours stretching ahead like a never-ending lagoon which threatens to wash over you until you are drowning in it. A moth flutters about in the room, desperately trying to get out, as if caught in a fishing net. You hear and see things that were always there and yet they look and sound different. Everything is more pronounced, like the swell of your breasts and the curve of your hips. The sun accentuates the fiery glow of the mountains and everything it touches. You try to find comfort in the little things. You step into the daylight, but the sun blinds you and the tide smells like blood. Mama brings you a freshly picked mango. The overpowering scent of the overripe fruit makes you feel sick. Eat, she says, but you can't. Every bite is a sweet little lie.

# 50

Tomorrow is my sixteenth birthday, but I don't feel festive. I don't feel anything at all. Sweet sixteen, they say. But there's nothing sweet about it. Even the cake that Mama will order from the pâtisserie will be at least two days old, and cost less than half of its original price. The icing on the cake will taste rancid. Instead of being light and fluffy, the heavy *massepain* will be like a stone in my stomach.

It's been weeks since Alexandre left without a word. I wonder if he ever thinks of me, even though we're oceans apart.

Whenever an Air Mauritius plane cuts across the clear blue sky, it's him that I think of. When I look deep into the sea, I see a reflection of his green eyes dancing in front of me. At Madame's house, I catch whiffs of his scent wherever I go. He has left traces everywhere. There are shadows of him in every room I enter – wherever I look. Sometimes I close my eyes and hear his voice whispering in my ears. I know he is gone and yet he still lives in my memory. In my dreams. Buried somewhere deep inside of me.

# 5 1

Sweat coats my entire body like oil. I move slowly through the lagoon with my arms wide open, and close my eyes. Burning, I dive into the sea stark naked. I want Alexandre to swim over and join me in the water. To swim around in circles, orbiting me. To touch me. To kiss the back of my neck. To pull me up against him. I want to wrap my legs firmly against his glistening body and not let go. I want him to carry me on his shoulders into deep waters I cannot reach. To anchor me. To take me in his arms.

But I know he won't. He's got her. One of his own. I never was. Never will be.

I open my eyes and all the pain comes at once, in a deluge. Drowning me. I want to close my eyes and forget.

# 5 2

I didn't think anyone at school would know about my birthday, a day like any other day in Riambel. But just before leaving, Mrs Maggie walks by my desk and slips a small packet wrapped in plain brown paper into my hands.

Open it later, she whispers.

I open my bag and slide it in between my thin Atlas note-books. Intrigued at the unexpected gift, I hold my bag close to my chest and wade through a tide of noisy kids towards the corner shop. Once outside, I tear open the paper wrapping to reveal a brand new diary. It has a silky turquoise cover decorated with tiny white orchids. The design is similar to the prints I've seen on the high-necked oriental dresses sold in China Town.

*For Noemi*
   *A little something to help you write. I look forward to reading your herstory.*
   *Happy sixteenth birthday!*
   *Yours*
      *Maggie*

Her neat handwriting is nicely looped and sophisticated, unlike my childish scribbles. Whenever I reluctantly hand her a sample of my writing, she nods encouragingly. Last term, I scribbled a few *sirandann* – word riddles in Creole – which she said nice things about. The fact that she made such an effort to learn our language instead of the language of the colonisers inspired me – making me want to learn more.

Next time there's a competition I'll make sure to enter your work, Noemi! she said, with a warm smile.

I didn't know what to say, so I stared at my feet instead. As if I had any chance. My rag of words, in a competition? Surely she must be kidding?

Then again, Mrs Maggie never jokes about these things. Nor would she ever laugh at us like the other teachers often do.

I like to think that she means her words, because deep down I really want to believe her. To think that perhaps there is a tiny chance that I might leave this dump one day. A sliver of hope like a ray of light shining in through my window at night. Lifting me from the fog that shrouds the *cité*. Casting a beam on my narrow little bed where I like to jot down random thoughts before drifting off to sleep.

Just because no one in my family has ever read a book it doesn't mean that I shouldn't spend my spare time reading. Or scribbling away. Thanks to Mrs Maggie and Misie Ravi, books have become my only friends.

I delicately pass my hand over the cover of the notepad, just for the pleasure of its silky feel. It is beautiful to touch and kind on the eye, with a seamless layout. I hold it to my face and breathe in the fresh smell of paper. The scent of hope and ink, smudged by warm tears running down my face. Erasing Mrs Maggie's words. Soaking the page like a dark cloud. The ink bleeding over the waterlogged paper. I try to clean up the mess by wiping it with my fingers, but I end up ripping the page, leaving behind a few empty words.

# 53

I watch the sun sink into the ocean and the colour drain out of the sky, bleaching it white.

# 54

What do you want to do?

I shrug and look out of the window. The shrieks of the neighbouring children playing *lamarel* on the street reach me.

You want to keep it?

It wouldn't be the first bastard born, would it? *Enn ti zanfan batar.* I turn to face Mama.

I've often heard Grand-mère talk of all those white men on the estate fathering a string of mixed-race kids. Eagerly sowing their seeds. Docile workers. On the plantation. Fertile ground. A factory.

But you haven't even finished school. How would you raise this child?

I'll manage.

You're a kid yourself!

I don't respond.

Look. I know someone—Mama doesn't finish her sentence.

It's still early enough, she continues. She can give you something to provoke contractions, so it'll be like a *fos kous*. You drink it and you won't feel the pain. It'll be over in no time.

How do you know? I look at her pointedly.

She avoids my gaze and slaps an unsuspecting mosquito on her leg. The insect is killed immediately, leaving a trace of glistening red against her black calf.

There's a woman called Tantine Ginette who lives in Rivière des Anguilles. I'll make arrangements for her to take care of it.

We can go there on a Sunday and come back in a taxi so you don't have to walk afterwards.

Looking at Mama's tired face, I find my insides struggling. Wrestling with wanting to be a mother to bring this mulatto baby into the world and carry it through life. Another bastard child.

I wish Marie could be here to tell me that it'll be all right.

I'm scared and alone.

# 55

Mama says there's a cyclone approaching the island. Just before a hurricane, all the animals that are able to leave flee somewhere else. You see the birds fly out of the storm, beating their wings. Seeking refuge. Far away from the winds and the torrents threatening to wash over us.

# 56

I'm all alone in the middle of a turbulent storm. Flimsy barracks with doomed roofs flying about. Thunder and lightning. A spear streaming straight for me. Like a flash of white about to strike.

# 57

W e're standing in front of Tantine Ginette's *lakaz* in Rivière
des Anguilles. The concrete house that's never been
painted looks abandoned. I nervously eye the plastic bottles and
old tyres piled up in a messy heap near the entrance.

Are you sure this is her place? I ask Mama.

Yes, she nods. She's expecting us.

A few minutes after we've knocked on the door, we hear
something stir inside. Something comes to life, and she walks
out looking over our shoulders.

*Bonzour.* She ushers us into the dark corridor that smells of
mildew and rain and quickly locks the door behind us. The whole
place feels damp. The walls are lined with several cracks where
greenish traces of water have left their marks.

Tantine Ginette is all bones and skin. Her eyes are unfath-
omably dark. We sit in front of her altar and watch her light a
candle that flickers to life. She kneels down and starts reciting
a few words.

*Oh mystère des cieux! Visitez-moi. Oh mystère des cieux! Visitez-
moi. Aidez cette jeune fille avec son enfant. Venez à notre secours!
Je vous en prie.*

*Oh mystery of the heavens! Help this girl with child. Come to our
rescue! I beg you.*

Over and over, she chants as if in a trance, until her eyelids
begin to flutter.

And then her eyes open up, wild and wide. I almost jump with
fright, but Mama pats my hand to reassure me. Tantine Ginette

looks at us as if she's seeing us for the first time. Her voice is different, not really sounding like her – as though there's suddenly another person in the room.

I shudder as she begins to utter a few words in a strange mix of patois. Unusual words from another era. I've never seen or heard anything like it before. Like someone else vibrating in her – taking over her body and voice. Dropping to the floor, she starts to roll around chanting as if possessed.

Mama, let's go, I whisper. She's frightening me.

Shush! Don't be scared. She's just communicating with the other side. Our ancestors who are here to guide us. We seek their help in times of trouble. They don't harm us. Their spirits protect us.

*Ena enn maler pe rod-rode otour sa tifi la. Fer bien atansion! Li pou koup ou lavi sinon!*

I see a spirit of the dead lurking dangerously close. They're looking for something. A life that's been taken away. Something that was rightfully theirs. They want to claim it back. I see water. Lots of water, and I see a pool of blood.

*Tansion ena mofinn!* Be careful. Be very careful.

I look at Mama and start to shake violently. I am cold, despite the tropical heat.

The woman's scaring the hell out of me. I want to run out of this mad place as fast as I can.

Je suis fatiguée
Je ne veux plus servir les dieux
Parce que ma peau est basanée
J'ai le sang encré, vous le sang bleu

Il n'y a rien d'ensoleillé
Dans cette affaire qui dure
Des jours, des mois et des siècles
Se mettre à genou pour des maîtres

Sous un ciel couleur de cendres
On a pas fini de nous vendre
Permettez-moi de fermer les yeux
Pour que je puisse oublier

Je ne veux plus y penser
A ce passé qui ne cesse de me hanter
Je vous ai aimé, vous m'aviez laissé tomber
Je ne suis qu'une petite fille d'esclavés

I'm tired
I don't want to be serving gods no more
Because my skin's ebony-dark
My blood's inky, but yours is blue

There's nothing sunny
About any of all these goings-on
Days, weeks, centuries
Bowing and scraping for masters

Under an ashen sky
There's no end to us being sold off
Just let me shut my eyes
So that I can forget

I don't want to think about it no more
About this past hanging over me
I loved you, you just dumped me
All I am's a little slave girl

# 58

I wake up screaming from my nightmare. Furiously kicking my bed. My face and neck feel hot. Hotter than the day. And I smack the angry mosquitoes that are biting my arms and legs. Sucking the blood out of me.

# 59

Two days later, Mama and I are back at Tantine Ginette's house. Drink this, Tantine orders. Her fingers are long and thin like bones.

My hands shake as I take the steel tumbler from her and sniff it suspiciously. I look at her questioningly.

Although her old brown face is lined with deep wrinkles, it's hard to guess her age. She has no eyelashes left, making her grey marble eyes look unusually big on her small face. Her frizzy hair's tied back and she wears a red scarf over her head.

What's in it?

It's just a tisane.

It smells of alcohol, I tell her. Is it medicine?

It's a concoction of natural herbs and a drop of rum. It's to numb the pain.

Come on. Drink up. It'll also give you strength. The quicker we start, the quicker it'll be over and done with.

How many times have you done this before?

Too many years for me to remember, and before that I watched my mama do it. Her mama did it too. Don't worry. I know what I'm doing. Afterwards, you'll thank me for it. Believe me. She rubs her wrinkled hands and arms with cologne and pats them dry with a towel.

Reluctantly, I gulp the disgusting liquid in one go and pull a face.

Good, she says, holding a long knitting needle in one hand and a piece of cloth in the other.

How long does it take?

It'll only be a minute or two. Put this cloth into your mouth, between your teeth, and scream into it if you must. But not too loud! Otherwise the neighbours will get suspicious and I'll get arrested.

I do as I'm told and close my eyes. Never in my entire life has a minute felt so long.

The cold piece of metal pokes around between my legs before entering me. Pushing upwards and deep inside. Instinctively my legs want to close, but a pair of strong hands is pinning me down – spreading them open like a human starfish glued to the bed. Swiftly, the metal penetrates my womb like a dangerous weapon and I flinch. A twist and a strong pull. My womb contracts at the unwelcome intrusion. Stabs of raw pain. I shake and I scream into the cloth. The pointed edge. Scraping my womb clean. A sore, tender stomach.

Almost there! Tantine announces. I just have to make sure there's nothing left behind.

I can barely hear her through the pain.

The agony is tearing me apart. Butchering my insides. After what feels like an eternity, there's blood running down my thighs. On the sheets. I see a clot of red attached to the surgical instrument dripping with blood. A piece of flesh. A small lump of meat. The ratlike carcass covered in slime. My dead baby.

The bleeding doesn't stop. It flows like a river. Gripped with pain, I bite into the cloth. I cry hot tears while my body cries fresh blood. I sweat profusely. Vomiting. Like a child, I wet the bed.

Everything's gushing out of me. From my pores. From my eyes. From every orifice.

My vision becomes blurry. I hear Tantine talking fast.

This isn't good. The bleeding. It should've stopped by now. Her mouth quivers into a deep frown.

I need more clean towels. Go. Get some. Quick! she shouts.

Looking down, I see the thick, red liquid flowing out of me. I want to vomit up my insides but there's nothing left.

She's bleeding like a beheaded pig. This has never happened before.

What? Hospital? No! Are you crazy? You know I can't take her to hospital. They'll ask too many questions and I'll go to prison.

Everything goes dark. The room closes in on me. I'm drowning in a black sea of blood.

# 60

Tantine Ginette doesn't want anything to happen to me while I'm still in her house.

You have to leave before it gets worse, she urges.

Mama gathers me in her arms. She carries me like a child, with a bloody towel stuck between my legs, and bundles me into the taxi. I drift in and out of consciousness. A few hours later, the bleeding hasn't stopped. I'm delirious with fever, and the infection turns my skin a purplish blue colour. Mama manages to find a doctor who apparently has just graduated from a university in India, and who is willing to do a home visit without asking too many questions. The young Muslim doctor wears an *horni* around her face. Perhaps she doesn't want to be seen entering the *cité*. No place for a respectable doctor. She gives a me dose of antibiotics and strong painkillers that knock me out.

This should help, but make sure she gets plenty of fluids in this abominable heat. Call me if there are any other complications, she tells Mama, in a voice full of concern and a sliver of fear.

I fold into a foetal position and turn my head to face the wall. Buried underneath the sheets, I close my eyes and curl around the hurt. I don't hear Mama's reply as she leads her out. The young doctor never comes back, because Mama can't afford to send for her again. When the medicine runs out, Mama makes me a concoction of moringa and ayapana leaves.

Drink up, Noemi. This will help heal the wounds and control the bleeding. She drops some brown sugar into the brew. But no amount of sugar can get rid of the bitter aftertaste.

# 6 1

I open my eyes. There's something blurry hovering above me. I can hear Mama shuffling about before entering my room.

She hands me a bowl of scrambled eggs clumped with rice.

Eat, she orders. You're nothing but a lump of skin and bones, she says.

In one brusque movement, she pulls open the flimsy curtains. Daylight hurts my eyes.

I'm off to work.

She goes out and leaves me alone to endure the silence. Reluctantly, I skim the belly of my bowl with the spoon, scooping out the mushy contents. Sliding the cold steel into the hollowness and emptying it all out. The taste of sand in my throat.

When Mama's gone, I draw the curtains and let the darkness creep back into the room like fog.

# 62

Unable to concentrate on my exams, I stop going to school. Mama says I should not leave without a school certificate, but what's the point?

I sleep during the day and stay up at night, never seeing daylight. When I remember to eat I dunk a few dry manioc biscuits in black tea the colour of gangrene. I forget about the trees and the birds and the sun in the sky. Every day's just the same.

# 63

I close my eyes. I am falling off the cliff in Souillac. Dropping into the depths of the ocean where the sounds are muffled. The bottom of the sea is full of strange, misshapen creatures with magnified eyes swimming blindly into an ocean of black silt. Suddenly, the water turns red and begins to spin into a baby storm – until it gets sucked down by an invisible force. Pulled into the bottom of the ocean. Buried.

*I am suffocating*
*I can't breathe*
*Kneeling, praying, begging, please!*

*I suffocate under your weight*
*Have some mercy*
*Let me breathe*

*You take away my right to live*
*As if my life doesn't matter*
*I wasn't born with privilege*

*My mama served your lady mama*
*Your papa lynched my papa*
*My sister bore your bastard baba*

# 64

I am all alone – marooned on an island of my own from which there's no escape.

*You decide to leave the confines of your room to see the ocean. The salty air clears your head. Your thoughts wander to an unknown continent, far away. A wave of hot air rises from the sand. The air is filled with the smell of the tide. Knocked out by the heat, you close your eyes for a minute trying to imagine a different life, but you're anchored here. You make small, tentative steps. There's something slippery under your sole – the remains of a dead fish tangled in seaweed. Buried in a cemetery of algae. The stench of decay fills your nostrils. You want to escape, but you can't. Where to? The horizon follows you wherever you go. Watching your every step. Your every move. Your every breath, until it stifles you and you can no longer breathe.*

# 65

Noemi, watch out. You've become your own enemy.

Days blend into nights. Nights blend into days. Day in. Day out. Morning turns into evening. And you still look like a fright. A day turns into a week. A week turns into a month. How long has it been? It's hard to say. You give yourself away. To whoever's willing to pay. For your cravings. Come. It's now down to 200 rupees. Just enough for the shot those blueish veins are dying for. Bulging and throbbing. Pulsing with thirst and need. A lethal cocktail. To get you through another day. You've sold yourself to the devil. But what does it matter? It's just a body anyway. An empty vessel.

# 66

Sometimes I drag my bare feet to the shore, as it feels somehow comforting to go back to the old and the familiar. To let the waves spray my face. To close my eyes and taste the sea. To let go – even if only for a moment.

One day, I see a family playing on the beach. The father and the mother are sunbathing while their two children are building sandcastles. There's something familiar about the man. His tallish figure – the way he turns his head.

From his mannerisms, I know it's him. I would have recognised Alexandre in a million. The way he carries himself with entitlement, as if the whole world belongs to him. The years may have added a few kilos here and there and a splash of grey to his hair, otherwise nothing's changed. I walk past him as he rubs sunscreen on his wife's freckled skin. He doesn't even notice me. Why would he? I am nobody.

I want to kick their perfect sandcastle, but I manage to restrain myself. I turn around, but the little girl looks up and I catch the fright in her clear blue eyes.

# 67

I grab a handful of sand and watch the white dust fall through my dirty fingers which are as black as coal. This makes me laugh out loud, but my laugh sounds hollow – without any joy. *Rire en belle.* Riambel.

Uncontrollably, I laugh again and again. Riambel. *Rire de plus belle.* It resonates loudly. The scream of a madwoman, the villagers will later call it.

As if in a trance, I walk towards the sea and let the frothy waves coil around my ankles like sea serpents. My bare feet a snarl of cuts. My toenails are broken seashells – rough and yellow.

There's no one in sight. I'm a lump of black against the white sandy beach. A shadow.

I enter into the lagoon fully dressed – my flabby arms raised in prayer.

The water embraces me. I turn my face towards the clear blue sky and let the waves carry me. The ocean roars and rumbles as if it were also laughing. At me or with me? I don't care. I'm cackling. The filao trees are singing and dancing in the breeze. We're all laughing together. One big orchestra. I hear the call of the sea. The lure of the mermaid. The chant of death ringing in my ears.

Riambel.

Ri-am-bel.

*Rire en belle.*

*Rire de plus belle.*

Suddenly, I stop laughing and start to cry. A stream of salty tears running freely down my face. And then I let go. My hands are loose and spread open in the water, with the palms up. A sea of relief.

*Dans la nuit accomplie et d'azur constellé,*
*La rumeur de la mer était la voix de l'ombre,*
*Et la fraîcheur de l'eau mélodieuse et sombre*
*Exhalait un parfum où j'aspirais, mêlé*
*Au sel marin, le miel des senteurs végétales.*
*Et l'amour avait pris le visage du soir,*
*Et l'amour nous chantait la chanson du flot noir…*
*Et, dans la fusion de ces douceurs égales,*
*Familières à l'ombre et qu'ignore le jour,*
*Nous étions si troublés que nous ne savions guère*
*Qui, de la nuit ou de la mer ou de l'amour,*
*Exhale le plus d'ombre et le plus de lumière.*

Within the spangled ultramarine night,
The ocean's whisper was the shadow's will
The dusky, rhythmic waves of water's chill
Released a brume in which I sensed the bite
Of sea salt, a bouquet of lush verdure.
And love had borrowed evening for its face,
And love sang us the tide, deep-hued and bass…
And, in the swirl of manifold pleasure
That shadows knew but day did not dream of,
Adrift were we who strained for some insight
Into which among the three – night, sea, and love –
Exudes the most of shade, the most of light.

ROBERT-EDWARD HART, 'La Beauté multiple'
(translated by Jeffrey Zuckerman)

# MAURITIAN WRITERS AND ARTISTS
# WHOSE WORK APPEARS IN *RIAMBEL*

## JEAN FANCHETTE (1932–1992)

Jean Fanchette was a renowned Mauritian poet, psychoanalyst and publisher who co-founded the bilingual literary journal *Two Cities* (1959–1964) with Anaïs Nin. His work includes the poetry collections *Osmoses* (1954), *Les Midis du sang* (1956), *Archipels* (1958), *Identité provisoire* (1965), *Je m'appelle sommeil* (1977) and *La Visitation de l'oiseau pluvier* (1981). Fanchette also published his PhD thesis, *Psychodrame et théâtre moderne* (1971), and a novel, *Alpha du Centaure* (1975). *L'Île Équinoxe*, an anthology of his poems, appeared posthumously in 1993.

In 1992, Issa Asgarally suggested to the Mayor of Beau Bassin-Rose Hill that they create the Prix Jean Fanchette. The jury of this literary prize has been chaired by J.M.G. Le Clézio since 1999.

'Constat' from *L'Île Équinoxe* (Editions Stock, 1993) used by permission of Véronique Fanchette.

## ROBERT-EDWARD HART, OBE (1891–1954)

Robert-Edward Hart was a Mauritian poet who was born on 17 August 1891 in Port Louis and died on 6 November 1954 at Souillac, in the south of Mauritius. He enriched Mauritian literature with many poems, plays, speeches and chronicles. He was awarded the Prix Edgar Poe by the Maison de Poésie de France for a selection of poems he published under the title *Poëmes Solaires* (1937). In addition to numerous collections of poetry he also wrote a cycle of novels, *Pierre Flandre* (1928–36). In 1935, Hart was awarded a Médaille Vermeil de l'Académie française. He was awarded an OBE in 1949, and in 1953 was made a Chevalier de la Légion d'honneur. He spent the last thirteen years of his life at Le Nef ('the nave'), a bucolic coral-stone beach cottage.

'La Beauté multiple' from *L'Ombre Étoilée* (The General Printing & Stationery Cy. Ltd, 1924) used by permission of Stefan Hart de Keating.

## VIJAYA TEELOCK (1956)

Vijaya Teelock, GOSK, was until recently Associate Professor of History at the University of Mauritius and Head of the Centre for Research on Slavery and Indenture, which she founded in 2006 at the university. The aim was to create an interdisciplinary group of researchers from Mauritius and abroad working on labour migrations that have occurred in the Indian Ocean. She is a member of the International Scientific Committee of the UNESCO Slave Route Project as well as the vice-president of the International Scientific Committee of the Indentured Labour Route Project.

She has recently embarked on a new venture to look more deeply into the history of women in Mauritius, and is also a member of the board of directors of the Intercontinental Slavery Museum Mauritius, created in 2020.

Extract from *Bitter Sugar* (Mahatma Gandhi Institute,1998) used by permission of Vijaya Teelock.

## MILA GUPTA (1950)

Mila Gupta has worked as an art teacher in state secondary schools and has regularly exhibited her paintings in exhibitions in Mauritius and abroad. Her intensely dreamlike paintings use vivid colours reminiscent of the Mauritian flora and landscape, and aim to capture the beauty, harmony and tranquillity of nature. The painting reproduced with Mila's permission on the cover of *Riambel* symbolises Mauritius' commitment to the preservation of biological diversity.

# ACKNOWLEDGEMENTS

I wish to thank Anna Soler-Pont, my incredible agent, and the entire team at Pontas Literary and Film Agency.

My lovely publisher and editor Susie Nicklin, for believing in me, Honor Scott for her meticulous work, and Phoebe Barker and everyone at The Indigo Press involved in publishing my debut novel. *Riambel* could not have found a better home.

I am forever grateful to J.M.G. Le Clézio, Issa Asgarally, Davina Ittoo, and the municipality of Beau Bassin-Rose Hill for awarding my manuscript *Riambel* the Prix Jean Fanchette 2021.

Thank you also to the following:

Haddiyyah Tegally, for the French translation of *Riambel*, and Jeffrey Zuckerman for translating the poems into English for this edition. Their stunningly beautiful interpretations gave me goosebumps.

The University of Iowa's International Writing Program (Women's Creative Mentorship Project), for the opportunity to participate as an emerging female writer from Mauritius (courtesy of the US Department of State's Bureau of Educational and Cultural Affairs). I particularly wish to thank Cate Dicharry, Christopher Merrill and Allie Gnade, who made our stay in the US a truly memorable one, and my IWP Fall Residency alumna mentor, Shenaz Patel, who told me to trust my writing.

Barlen Pyamootoo, Tatiana de Rosnay and Ananda Devi, for all their encouragement. Lindsey Collen and Reshma Bholah, for the magical evenings at Riambel. Rebonto Guha, for the long lunches, Evelina Dietmann, for her invaluable advice, and Mark Casali, who said I should write with more emotion.

Ameerah Arjanee, Lisa Ducasse, Florence Guillemain, for their excellent feedback, and Yovan Mahadeb, who encouraged me to submit my manuscript to the Prix Jean Fanchette.

Vijaya Teelock, for her permission to cite her work, and Stefan Hart de Keating and Véronique Fanchette, for their permission to cite the work of Robert-Edward Hart and Jean Fanchette. Daniella Bastien, for her expertise in reviewing the Creole texts.

Gaitee Hussain, for her continuous moral support. Sara Hoffmann-Cumani and Claudio Cumani, for their compassion and for lifting me up when I was ill. Steffen Manske, who saved my life.

Transforming a manuscript into the book
you hold in your hands is a group project.

Priya would like to thank everyone
who helped to publish *Riambel*.

THE INDIGO PRESS TEAM

Susie Nicklin
Phoebe Barker
Honor Scott

JACKET DESIGN

Luke Bird

PUBLICITY

Jordan Taylor-Jones

EDITORIAL PRODUCTION

Tetragon
Gesche Ipsen
Sarah Terry

RECIPE TESTING

Geraldine Doolall